To B.
God b
Hope you
the book
Love + Prayers
Maryanne Raphael

Dancing on Water

A Novel by
Maryanne Raphael

Design & Computer work By Donald Johnson

Cover by J.R. Roosenberg

Special assistants Dr. Eve Jones & Pilar Toledo

This book is dedicated to my two grandchildren Zeal and Anjali

I wish to thank all of my friends who have encouraged me in my writing over the many years.

And a special thank you to NaNoWriMo.com for getting me to write a novel in one month.

J.R. Jean Roosenberg
2911 Sand Trap Rd. SE
Deming, New Mexico 88030
Jiniroos2@msn.com

Permission is given to reproduce my artwork of a white bird dancing on water for the book 'Dancing on Water' authored by Maryanne Raphael. All other copyrights to remain with the artist J.R. Jean Roosenberg.

J.R. Jean Roosenberg 04-20-09
J.R. Jean Roosenberg Date

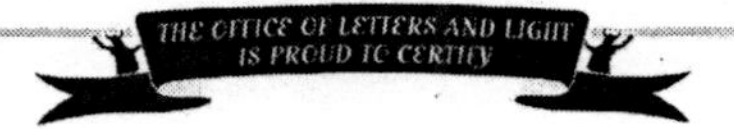

Maryanne Raphael
Novelist's name

author of

Dancing On Water
Novel title

a

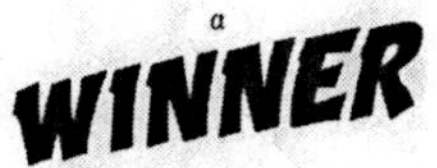

of the

2008 National Novel Writing Month contest

THROUGH STORM AND SUN, YOU TRAVERSED THE NOVELING SEAS. PITTED AGAINST A MERCILESS DEADLINE AND BATTLING HORDES OF DISTRACTIONS, YOU PERSEVERED. YOUR DEDICATION TO THE HIGH-VELOCITY LITERARY ARTS IS REMARKABLE. YOUR VICTORY SHALL BE RECORDED FOR ALL TIME IN THE ANNALS OF THE OFFICE OF LETTERS AND LIGHT, WHERE IT WILL SERVE AS A BEACON TO WRITERS HOPING TO SOMEDAY FOLLOW YOUR TRIUMPHANT PATH. YOU DID IT, NOVELIST. WE COULDN'T BE PROUDER.

Lindsey Grant, Community Liaison | **Chris Baty**, Director | **Tavia Stewart**, YWP Director

12/1/08
Date

Contents

At the heart of the storm
is a quiet promise
The deepest hunger brings
the recipe for Manna
The loneliest prisoner
finds Hope
hidden in his heart
if he goes deep enough.
The God of Rain and Death
lovingly caresses
his soul.
How can I keep from singing?

Chapter One
The Recipe for Manna

On September 23, 2007, Shannon Dunlap came face to face with her own death for the first time. She had thought of it many times in her life but it had seemed like a fragile nightmare that would disappear once she woke up. However, this time Death stood right in front of her, as real as anyone or anything she had seen in her life.

Long ago she had tried to make friends with her death, to see it as a natural part of life but it had been too ephemeral and she had let her mind wander to other subjects. Her Mexican friend, Juanita, had told her that Ash Wednesday was the time to learn to accept your death and she had gone to Mexico with her friend to attend the Ash Wednesday services.

It had astonished her to see that the churches in Mexico had many more people on Ash Wednesday than on Easter Sunday. Even when the priest had placed ashes on her forehead saying "Ashes to Ashes and dust to dust" she still felt as far from thoughts of death as she ever had.

Shannon had no idea why Death had come looking for her at this time. She was 60 years old but could easily pass for forty with her slender figure, thick light brown hair, young face with large violet eyes, turned up nose and sensual mouth that was usually smiling. She was in excellent health and had been all her life.

She looked closer, expecting to see that Death had faded away but Death looked deep into her eyes and smiled a dubious smile at her.

She remembered that her doctor had told her she was suffering from Alzheimer's, the disease that killed her mother. No wonder Death had come looking for her.

Shannon had heard that when someone died their whole life flashed before them. And sure enough her life was enfolding before her. She wouldn't say it was flashing. It was in slow motion with large gaps in between.

Her Grandmother Flanagan was lying in her big bed with the pink lace on the ceiling. She was saying, "If I can make it to springtime I know I can live until Christmas."

She saw Grandmother's beautiful fragrant flower garden, lilacs and roses and hollyhocks and petunias. She knew the flowers would help Grandmother stay alive until Christmas.

However, she soon found herself at Grandmother's wake. Grandmother was wearing her favorite dress, a powder blue silk with tiny roses. Her eyes were closed and Mother told Shannon Grandmother was going to sleep forever but she was happy because her soul was up in Heaven with Jesus and his Mother.

All of the family and close friends had gathered to celebrate Grandmother's birthday in Heaven. The men were drinking heavily and the women were eating huge plates full of food followed by cakes and pies and custards.

Shannon and her sister Jeanette were playing Old Maid with their cousins.

They were sitting on the floor in the living room right next to the casket where Grandmother Flanagan slept.

A car pulled up out front and Aunt Rose shouted, "It's Grandmother Moats and the Protestants!" Everyone rushed around the house hiding the alcohol and even made the children put the Old Maid cards away.

"We don't want to give the Moats a bad idea about us."

She knew the Moats already had a bad idea of her family because whenever she spent the night with Grandmother Moats she would pray, "Please let Louise and her family leave the wicked Catholic Church and return to the Methodists so we can all be in Heaven together."

What really confused her about the question of religion was when she went to Sunday school the nuns taught that only Catholics could go to Heaven. So Shannon didn't know whether she had it covered because she was being prayed for on both sides or would she luck out completely because whoever won a seat in Heaven might see her as part of those who couldn't make it.

Shannon found herself at five years old riding a horse on the Carousel at the County Fair. Her sister Jeanette was on the horse behind her and her mother and father were standing outside waving at the girls.

The music was pleasant in spite of the tinny tone. The air smelled of cotton candy and barbecue. The sound of laughter and excited conversation filled the air and Shannon wished her ride could go on forever.

After the Merry-go-around, the four of them stopped at a booth where Shannon's father threw some soft balls and won a large teddy bear for Jeanette and a doll as tall as she was for Shannon.

Shannon and Jeanette took tap dancing classes and their mother made them lovely pink costumes for the recital. As she danced, Shannon felt completely alive, filled with a joy she had rarely known before. "I want to be a dancer when I grow up. I want to feel this happiness and entertain people and help them be happy too."

When she was seven years old, Shannon took a walk in the fields behind their homes with her next-door neighbor Larry who was nine. They were holding hands and walking next to the railroad tracks when Larry said, "Let's run across while there is no train coming."

He dropped her hand and ran across.

Just as she started across she heard the train blow its horn and she was paralyzed. She stood staring in the direction of the train like a little deer in front of an oncoming car.

Larry screamed for her to get off the tracks but she could not move. As the train approached he jumped beside her and pushed her off the tracks, falling on top of her just as the train roared by.

"Don't tell anybody about this," Larry said. "The grownups will be angry because we were on the tracks. Let this train be our little secret." She never told anyone although she often felt herself back there staring at the oncoming train.

Shannon and Jeanette made their first Communion the same day. Jeanette seemed to like the idea, to enjoy choosing dresses and veils together but Shannon was disappointed. She had hoped to celebrate the grand occasion alone, to be the center of attention for once in her life.

When the big day came she forgot all her regrets. She admired herself in the mirror. "You will make a beautiful bride one day," she whispered.

She knew this was supposed to be a very spiritual day, a day when she really came to know Jesus. She was excited about this. "This is the most spiritual excitement I ever felt."

When she walked up to the altar to receive Communion her heart was beating rapidly. She prayed that she would be worthy.

The priest said, "Body of Christ," and she said,"Amen."

She had expected to hear beautiful music and feel ecstasy but she felt only disappointment. She begged Jesus to forgive her for not being able to care about this very special occasion.

Shannon's Grandfather Moats was a beekeeper. She loved to watch him tend his bees. She loved honey and Grandfather had taught her to be thankful to the bees. She begged him to let her go with him to visit them.

He said, "My bees are gentle and they know me and know that I wish them well. They know I am not afraid of them and they are not afraid of me but whenever anyone is afraid of them they become afraid and they attack."

Each time she visited Grandfather Moats she begged to visit the bees and promised she would not be afraid and would not frighten them.

One day he gave her his special protection outfit which was way too large for her and took her with him to the hives.

She was so proud. She kept thanking the bees for the delicious honey they had given her. She was surrounded by bees and they accepted her. Then she tripped and fell and while she was trying to get up the bees began stinging her and she panicked. Grandfather picked her up and took her inside.

She had been stung many times but she was not allergic so no real harm was done. She never again begged her grandfather to take her to visit the bees. "I still love them," she said, "And I thank them for the honey and I forgive them for stinging me but I don't want to visit them again."

Shannon liked school and was an excellent student. She tried out for cheerleader and was chosen. She loved the excitement of a ball game and the fun of leading cheers, dancing and doing acrobatics as the crowd applauded and accompanied her.

One day she put a red rinse on her hair so she would look special during the game. In the middle of the game a hard rain fell and the red from her hair ran down her face and arms. It was embarrassing. People thought she was bleeding and she had to explain what she had done.

Although her parents had decided she would have to wait until she was sixteen years old to begin dating, Shannon talked them into letting her go to a movie with her friend Larry. His father offered to accompany them as their chauffeur and chaperon.

Shannon felt grownup being out on a date. She liked Larry very much but she did not have any romantic feelings about him. They had been good friends since she was very young. She was happy that his father was accompanying them so there would be no chance for him to try to kiss her.

When she was sixteen Shannon fell in love for the first time. She had been reading a newspaper when she saw photos of soldiers fighting in Korea who wanted a pen pal. Airman Vincent Mooney looked quite handsome so she wrote him a letter. He answered right away and they had a great time writing back and forth. They shared their life stories with one another, their hopes and their dreams. Their plans and their goals.

By the time he had a leave and came back to the states, they were old friends and the love they already felt for one another was intensified at first sight. Vincent had only two weeks in Ohio because he wanted to go home to Michigan before he had to return to Korea.

Vincent hadn't realized Shannon was only sixteen years old because while she had told him much about her family, her childhood, her school, she had omitted that.

He gave her her first real kiss, one she would always remember. He was careful not to let their romance go too far because of her young age. But she hated to see him go and she knew her heart would never be the same. She prayed he would come home safely and they could get married and live happily ever after.

After he returned to Korea, they continued their letters. At first they were very passionate, making plans to get together. She wrote him every day and cried herself to sleep each night. Her prayers began with requests that he be kept safe and return to her.

But she got busy with school, cheerleading, dance classes and her letters got shorter and less frequent. She began dating boys in her school and her love for Vincent faded.

His letters were also less frequent and she answered them with cheerful news but avoided declarations of love or promises for the future.

Her old friend Larry started asking her out to dates again and she always went. He was her best friend, had been since they were both in kindergarten. They went to movies together and he took her to the prom, the most important dance of the year. She was just beginning to think of the possibility of romance with Larry when he graduated. He got a football scholarship to Ohio University in Athens Ohio. Larry was busy at college and did not come home very often.

Shannon was a junior in high school, president of the class, cheerleader and in charge of the class yearbook. In her senior year she was even busier.

She was Valedictorian of her graduating class and won a scholarship to Ohio State. She had never lived away from home before and the idea was both exciting and frightening.

Shannon majored in History with a minor in theater arts. She was in several school plays, playing Blanche Du Bois in Tennessee Williams's “Street Car Named Desire.” She was popular with the male students and had many dates. She was a good dancer and loved to go dancing.

She took a class in fencing and began to date her teacher, Juan Perez who had won the title of World Championship at the International Competition in Panama. Juan taught her how to fence and she was offered a job teaching beginners in the physical education department and she gave a class in the theater department.

She was given a Phi Beta Kappa gold key and won a Scholarship to the Sorbonne and a Fulbright travel grant.

When she graduated, Juan took her out to celebrate and then said goodbye and she never heard from him again.

She missed him very much and for a while she grieved his absence.

But her mind was soon completely occupied with her plans for her trip to Paris, the first time she had even left the United States. She wanted to travel light but she would be in Europe for at least one year and she would need clothes for all four seasons.

Shannon, Jeanette and their mother went shopping to make sure Shannon had all the clothes she would need for her time in Europe. Shannon had always thought of her sister Jeanette as much younger and a sort of playful pest but she had grown older now and Shannon found herself enjoying her company.

She had always worshiped her mother and enjoyed all the time they spent together. She realized she was going to miss her family while she was so many miles away for them. Even worse than the many miles was the many months they would be apart.

On September 28, 1960, Shannon sailed from New York City to Le Havre, France on the French line. As the ship pulled out to sea the orchestra played "California, Here I Come" and for a few minutes Shannon was sure she was on the wrong ship.

Shannon had agreed to have a roommate to share her cabin, not only because it made the trip less expensive but also because she didn't want to feel lonely leaving her family for the first time.

Her cabin mate was an attractive young American woman named Carrie who had been living in Europe for many years. She seemed to enjoy answering all of Shannon's questions about France.

One day Shannon returned to the cabin and was surprised to find Carrie in tears.

"What's wrong?" she asked.

"Oh, I'm so sorry you caught me crying. I didn't want to bring you down but two weeks ago my fiancé died in a hang gliding accident. He had been hang gliding for years. We were supposed to get married next month."

Carrie took a Kleenex from the table and wiped her face.

Shannon put her arms around Carrie. "I am so sorry," she said.

"Let's go play badminton," Carrie suggested, starting out of the cabin.

Shannon followed her.

The days at sea went rapidly. There were always interesting activities and Shannon made many new friends. The meals were exquisite, gourmet foods served with excellent style. The linen table clothes, lovely flowers and delicate wines made each meal an occasion to remember. She loved the way there were so many delicacies and such a dainty quantity of each.

Shannon woke up at five a.m. on the morning the ship arrived in Le Havre.

She dressed and went to stand on the deck. Many passengers were there waiting.

She could see the shores of France and was surprised to see many grown men and women riding on their bikes.

The first time she saw Paris Shannon was overwhelmed. She had never thought she would fall in love with a city but she did. The only thing that kept her from deciding to spend the rest of her life in that beautiful city was the fact that her family was so far away and she knew she would never be able to convince them to move here.

Shannon got herself a room at the Cite Universitaire where students from all over the world could live as long as they could show they were students. She hoped to get a room in the French house so she could speak French most of the time but it was full so she ended up at the American house.

When she visited the Eiffel Tower she loved its shape but the color looked like rust to her. However, the view of the city from the top of the tower filled her with joy. She was enchanted to learn that the Moulin Rouge, made famous by Toulouse Lautrec, still had dancers doing the Cancan.

She loved visiting the wonderful old churches, Notre Dame, Sacre Coeur Basilica, Sainte Chapelle. Their Gothic structure and brilliant stained glass gave her the sense of awe, bliss and peace she always felt at the ocean.

When Shannon went to the Sorbonne to register she had many surprises. The good news was that a year's tuition was less than one hundred American dollars. But she was disappointed to learn that French universities did not have a catalogue where a student could choose classes and learn when they met. She had to go to a large hall lined with bulletin boards where professors notified students when and where and what classes would be available. It seemed that French professors had handwriting resembling doctors and since they were in French it was even more difficult for her to decipher the little piece of paper stuck to the bulletin boards.

Student meals were only one franc which was approximately a quarter and they included a bottle of white or red wine. The only part of the meal that bothered Shannon was the fact that they were served horsemeat most of the time. At first she thought it was beef but it was like leather.

On the first day of class Shannon was overwhelmed by the size of her classroom. A French student told her that the Sorbonne dated back to the Middle Ages. The benches were all made of marble. She learned that students were not required to attend class. They could come to every class if they wished or never come if they did not wish to hear the professor. No one took attendance. There were no examinations, no papers due in individual classes.

Anyone who wished to get a diploma had to sign up for a particular test that was given several times a year by the University. Shannon chose the classes that appealed to her and decided to attend every day. After all she had come all this way to learn about France.

Shannon's roommate at the American House was Helga Schneider from Germany. Helga spoke excellent French and passable English. They decided to speak together in French so Shannon could perfect the language.

One day Shannon entered the room and found Helga talking on the phone in German. She looked upset that Shannon had entered the room and she hurriedly hung up the phone. A short time later Helga left the room and did not return until the next day.

Shannon wondered if she had a boyfriend but Helga seemed so private about the situation she didn't ask her anything.

Another day Shannon returned home to find Helga speaking rapidly with three Algerian students. As soon as they saw Shannon, the visitors said goodbye and left without even being introduced.

Then one night when Shannon had made plans to see a play with a friend but she got an upset stomach and came home, she found Helga and her friends putting guns into boxes.

"What in the world is going on?" asked Shannon.

"I'm so sorry," Helga said. "Sit down, Shannon, I want to tell you what's happening in France today."

While Helga talked her friends continued packing guns.

Shannon was terrified.

"Do you know that Algeria is fighting for their independence from France?"

"This is the first I'm hearing of it," Shannon said.

"Don't you read the newspapers?"

"No. I have so many books to read I haven't read a newspaper since I got here."

"I know you love France and respect French people. You don't know what is going on in Algeria. The French soldiers are massacring the people, raping the women, torturing and killing civilians, burning houses with people inside, bombing hospitals and schools."

"Oh, I hope that isn't true." Shannon said.

"I wish it wasn't true," Helga said. "I have friends who were tortured by the French and whose families were killed. That's why I got involved."

"No matter what is going on, I hate the idea of having guns in my home."

"We won't do it again. Something came up at the last moment. We had a chance to deliver some weapons and we had to get them ready."

"You know, Shannon, the French army has been behaving like the Gestapo, doing all kinds of terrible things to innocent people."

"It makes me ill to hear about such things," Shannon said, "But you and I are guests of the French government and I don't think we are the ones to correct the situation."

The next day Shannon read every newspaper she could find. And she got the French army's side of the story. The first articles said the French army had a campaign of pacification of what was still considered at the time to be a part of France. The "café wars" resulted in nearly 5000 deaths in France between the two rebel groups though the years of the Algerian war for independence. An estimated million people died in Algeria during this time.

De Gaule's return to power was supposed to ensure Algeria's continued occupation and integration with the French Community. But De Gaule progressively shifted in favor of Algerian independence which he saw as inevitable. He organized a vote of the Algerians. They chose independence. De Gaule pronounced Algeria an independent

country on July 3, 1962. The Oran massacre four days after the vote proved that the war was not over. Within a year, a million refugees, most of the Jewish community and many pro-French Muslims left Algeria.

Shannon had always liked Albert Camus' books. She learned that he was born in Algeria and wanted to see his country independent from France even though he spent much time there.

Helga had been careful not to mention the war again and to keep all war related activities out of their room.

Then a few weeks later, she invited Shannon to join her at her desk for a glass of wine. As they drank, Helga said, "I've noticed you reading about the war. I was just wondering if you might like to help us. It would just be for one time. We have to get these guns through Spain and into Algeria. We were thinking since you are an American if you traveled with us the officials would be likely to think we were tourists. Could you help us get arms to the people fighting for their independence?"

"I'm sorry," Shannon said. "I don't believe in any war. Please don't ask me again and please don't bring any more guns into our room."

Helga promised she would not bother her again. And a few days later she disappeared and Shannon never saw her again.

Shannon read in the paper: "There is no History of the Algerian War. There are a multitude of histories and personal paths through it. Everyone involved lived through it in their own way. "

Every dog can claim his day
But night belongs
to stray cats
who prowl dark streets
looking for a home
over there
safe from
canine cadence.

Chapter Two
All The Dogs in Europe Bark

Shannon signed up to take an important test at the Sorbonne so she could get a Superieur diploma. The topic was French civilization and teaching French abroad. She had been faithfully attending many classes on this subject so she knew she had a good chance of passing.

She was taking a course in pronunciation at the Institute de Phonetique and her teacher was very helpful. Margarite Faison was an actress at the Comedie Francaise in addition to being an excellent teacher. She was very dramatic, speaking with her arms and tossing her long red hair over her shoulder. She always dressed in black, choosing elegant dresses that showed off her slender figure without being flamboyant.

Margarite was excited to learn that Shannon was taking the examination and she helped her choose a poem and make sure every sound had the proper accent.

There were several other students taking the test and Margarite told them they must study very hard and work

diligently on their accents. She described the examination. "The first half of the test is oral. Dr. Fouchet who wrote the book on Phonetics will sit at the table with his head down so he cannot see the student. If he can tell by your accent what country or what part of France you come from you automatically fail the test and he sends you out of the room.

"Your French does not have to be perfect but you have to work on the problems that people of your nationality or province have with the language. If you solve those problems you can be excused for not sounding perfect."

Shannon went to the Sorbonne on the morning of the examination. There was a large crowd of students waiting to take the test. A woman holding a box came up to each student and allowed him or her to reach into the box and take a number. "That number decides the order in which you take the test."

Shannon was disappointed to see that she would have a long wait. She had picked number 675. The young man next to her exclaimed, "Mon dieu, I have number one."

"I'll trade you," Shannon said quickly.

The man gladly traded numbers with her.

Before Shannon had a chance to panic, a woman came out the main door and shouted, " Nombre un! (Number one)!"

Shannon followed the woman inside. They went down a long hall and into a huge room where eight professors were sitting at a long table. Just as her Phonetic teacher had said, Mr. Fouchet had his head down so that he could not see her.

She rejoiced when her favorite teacher, Marguerite, jumped up and began directing her with her arms as though she were leading an orchestra. Shannon had often had problems knowing when to raise or lower her voice when speaking French. With her teacher directing her she relaxed and was able to remember all the words she needed.

All of the teachers except Mr. Fouchet took turns asking her questions. Without seeming to care whether the

other teachers liked it or not, Marguerite kept directing Shannon in her accents.

When her time was finally up and the teachers thanked her and excused her Shannon felt a wonderful relief.

She felt confident she had passed her orals and now all she had to do was pass the written test.

Shannon had no trouble passing the 4 hour written examination since she found it so much easier to read and write French than it was to speak it without a noticeable accent.

It was announced that the test results would not be known for several months.

Shannon's scholarship money was ending soon and she did not want to return to America. She had fallen in love with France and wanted to remain as long as she could so she began looking for a job.

An American student told Shannon that the U.S. Air Force was advertising for Recreation Directors and Entertainers for the Service Club in Evreux, France, which was only a few hours ride from Paris.

Shannon took the train to the small town of Evreux and took a taxi to the Air base.

The woman who interviewed her was tall and thin, about 50 years old with dyed black hair, white powder on her face and bright red lipstick. She wore a light blue uniform and stockings with a black line down the back.

"I'm Mrs. Kline," the woman said, shaking Shannon's hand.

Shannon handed her a copy of her resume. The woman studied it carefully and said, "So you studied at the Sorbonne! I guess you speak good French."

"My French isn't perfect," Shannon said, "But I can say anything I want to say in French and I can usually understand anything anyone says to me."

"That's important," Mrs. Kline said, "We often need to communicate with people in the economy."

"Can you sing or dance?" she asked.

"I studied tap dancing for many years and danced in many recitals."

When Shannon was offered the job, she felt confused. She had wanted to get a job in order to remain in Europe but if she was working and living on the base it would be more like living in the United States than living in Paris. Yet she knew it was difficult for a foreigner to get a job in France so if she wanted to stay here this was probably her only chance. She accepted the job.

Leaving Paris was difficult for Shannon. She has never felt so attached to any place in her life. Beautiful Luxemburg gardens were right across from Cite Universitaire where she lived. The River Seine seemed so romantic. The little bookstores on the shore across from Notre Dame cathedral had been one of her favorite spots. To walk down the Champs Elysee was such an adventure. The people of Paris were like no others that she had ever seen. Many of them traveled by bicycle no matter where they went.

Most of the French women she knew had a very limited wardrobe compared to American women but they always looked elegant.

She loved to visit the Louvre and look at the Mona Lisa, the Winged Victory, and all the other magnificent works of art. She enjoyed the Impressionist Museum, the Jeau de Paume, even more where she admired works by Monet, Manet, Van Gogh, Gauguin etc.

She enjoyed listening to French songs on the radio and watching French movies. She wondered if she would have access to them on the base or if everything would be in English.

Tears slipped down her cheeks as she sat alone in the train going to Evreux with all the possessions she had in Europe. "Will I ever see Paris again?" she thought. "Of course I will. I took this job so I could stay close to Paris. I will go to Paris every week on my days off." She felt better once she made that decision.

Shannon sat back and watched the scenery go by.

When she arrived at the air base in Evruex she was taken to the Service Club where Mrs. Kline gave her some papers to fill out and explained her job to her.

A tall pretty woman with short black curly hair and big blue eyes outlined with heavy makeup was sitting at a desk. She wore a uniform just like Mrs. Kline's.

"Shannon, this is Bobby. She is the worker you are replacing." Bobby stood up and leaned over to shake hands. "I'll be here for a few more days and I'll help you get started."

Bobby told her, "You have a choice between living in the Officers' barracks and renting a place in the town. You can have a room in the officers' quarters while you decide where you want to be."

The officers' quarters, called the B.O.Q., reminded her of the four years in the dormitory at Ohio State and the year in the students' housing at the Cite Universite so she knew right away that she wanted to rent a room with a French family. She looked forward to practicing her French all the time.

Bobby took her to the officer's dining room. There was quite a good variety of food available. Shannon hadn't had a hamburger since she left the United States so she enjoyed one with ketchup, relish, potato salad and strawberry short cake for dessert.

Two school teachers joined them for the meal. They talked all during the meal, petty base gossip that did not interest Shannon since she didn't know any of the people whose reputations were being destroyed. If there was any truth to what they were saying every man on the base was sleeping with every woman in a wild game of musical chair.

The women were especially hard on the base commander's wife. It seems she was a luscious blond, about twenty-five with a great figure, a red sports car, and two miniature poodles that never left her side. She got her exercise climbing in and out of bed with all the airmen.

"You can't blame her too much," the older of the two teachers said very seriously as she stuffed a bite of steak into her mouth "She's young and pretty and he's over fifty."

"I don't know how she ever got mixed up with such an old foggy," the other said as she sipped her coke.

"I guess he makes a lot of money being commander of the whole base," the other teacher said. "A girl like that needs a man with money. She needs pretty clothes."

"Surely she could find a rich civilian," the younger teacher said. "I can't see any girl living on a base by choice."

"We're here by choice," her friend reminded her.

"Well, we're not young and pretty. This is our only chance to see the world. But that woman could marry any rich man who wanted to traipse around the world in style."

"It looks like this is a pretty wild base," Shannon told Bobby.

"I've worked on several bases," she said. "They are all like this. People get tired of the base movies and there's nothing left to do but get drunk and have affairs."

Shannon returned to her room and began unpacking. The B.O.Q. was arranged so that every occupant had a room of his own that opened into a small kitchen from one door and a bathroom from the other, both of these were shared by the occupant next door.

After a few minutes, there was a knock at the door. A slender attractive black woman stood there. "I'm Ellie," she said. "I guess you're my new roommate. I mean we share the kitchen and bath."

"Glad to meet you," Shannon said.

"I hope you'll like it here better than I do," Ellie said with a smile.

"I don't think I'm going to like it, "Shannon said.

"Wait til you are here a while. It gets worse. But I did not come to scare you. I wanted to try to make you feel at home in this jungle."

Shannon invited Ellie to sit down and talk.

"Have you been here long?" she asked as she continued hanging up her dresses.

"Too long," Ellie said. "I'm moving off the base soon. I'm not getting transferred or discharged or anything beautiful like that. I am just renting an old mansion in town. It will be great just to be off the base and in a real French town. I'm a nurse and I work at the base hospital. But you're a civilian. Are you a teacher?"

"No, I'm going to be working in the Service Club."

"Can I help you unpack?" Ellie asked.

"There's not much more to do," Shannon said. "You can entertain me while I finish. Tell me about the base."

"The less said about the base the better," Ellie said, "You will know too much about it soon."

Ellie looked at her watch and said, "I've got to go. I have a date so I'd better go fix myself up a bit. I hope I didn't discourage you too much."

She had only been gone for ten minutes when Bobby knocked on her door.

"Are you ready for the party?" she asked. "There's one every night here."

Shannon was tired and didn't feel like a party but something told her it was part of her job and she didn't want to disappoint anyone on her first day.

The party was in full swing when they arrived. It was being held in the room of one of the officers. Bobby introduced him as Rich when he greeted them at the door. He was a tall, thin, quiet captain with a full smile and shy eyes.

Bobby knew everyone in the room and told them, "This is Shannon. She's replacing me at the service club."

The other service club worker was at the party. Marcella was a pretty blond singer from California who had once had her own television show. She resembled Peggy Lee.

"Glad to meet you," she said. "We need new blood here. Not that I'm glad Bobby is leaving. It's a shame we

can't all three run the club. It would be nice if Mrs. Klein was the one going."

Bobby introduced me to a handsome general about forty years old with slightly graying hair. "This is Van," she said.

"I'm the one taking Bobby away," he said.

"I love that big ape," Bobby said. "But I wish he weren't mixed up with the Air Force. I'm not hep on being an officer's wife. I'll have to mix with the other wives and they are such squares."

"You'll pep them up," Van said.

"I'm sure she will," Marcella said.

The host, Captain Rich, asked Shannon, "What would you like to drink?"

She asked for Scotch on the rocks.

"So much?" she asked.

"That's just a starter, Soon you'll be a drunk like the rest of us."

"I have to go to the bathroom!" Bobby announced. "So everyone make a lot of noise. Every time I get inside, it suddenly gets quiet and I get too inhibited to piss. So please keep talking and laughing until I come back so I can piss in peace."

When Bobby returned from the bathroom, she said, "I hate men! You fellows never put the top down on the toilet. It's so inconsiderate."

She put her arms around Van. "Please remember that I like the toilet seat down. I almost fell inside because someone left it up."

There was more laughter.

Captain Rich said, "Shannon, you're not drinking. That's against the law here on this base. It's drink or die. Come on, drink up!"

He poured himself another glass of Scotch and finished it in one drink. Shannon had never seen anyone drink as much as these people were drinking.

"I have to take my mind off my problems," he said. "You're not drinking because you just arrived. Wait til you've been here a while."

A dignified civilian, tall with green eyes and a small moustache came towards Shannon. "That's not fair, Rich," he said. "You're monopolizing our new girl."

He turned to Shannon, "Mind if I join you two?"

"Not at all," she said.

He pulled up a chair near the sofa where Shannon was sitting.

"I'm Walter Farrington. I represent the University of Maryland. It's my unpleasant duty to see that any airman who wishes to improve his mind has the opportunity. Only a few take advantage of the opportunity. Every time I get an airman who is really interested in learning he gets transferred before he has a chance. It seems the Air Force wants to keep the men as stupid as possible. I guess you can't blame them, the best soldier is a dumb soldier. Theirs is not to reason why. Theirs is just to do or die. There I go talking too much again"

"You don't have to apologize," Captain Rich said, "We expect an intellectual to rattle on like that. That's what sets you apart from all us dumb alcoholics."

A Johnny Mathis record was playing "A Certain Smile" and most of the people in the room were dancing. Walter invited Shannon to dance with him and she agreed.

When the song ended they returned to the sofa. Rich was gone so Walter sat on the sofa next to Shannon.

Bobby and Van made the rounds telling everyone good night. "It's Motel time!" Bobby shouted. Everyone laughed.

Bobby told Shannon, "I'll pick you up at a quarter to nine. Be ready because Mr. Klein is a stickler for promptness. But she's not hard to get along with once you learn her ways. I'll help you all I can. Good night!"

Walter walked her home to her room after the party.

He tried to talk her into going to his room for one last drink. But she was exhausted and she was not used to drinking.

The next morning Bobby drove Shannon to the service club. All of the buildings on the base were a sick shade of green and shaped like a shoebox. The service club was one of the larger buildings.

Bobby and Shannon had a cup of coffee at the snack bar which was connected to the service club. Then they went to Mrs. Klein's office. She was already busy behind her desk. She looked up when the women entered and smiled.

"Good morning, girls," she said. "Sit down, Shannon, and I'll tell you something about the club."

Bobby excused herself, "I have to check with the artist about some posters for the dance."

Mrs. Klein went into a long harangue about the importance of the club, how it was a real home for so many homesick airmen and what a great responsibility it was for the women who ran it.

She gave Shannon a tour of the club. There was a large lounge and a tiny kitchen where the service club workers prepared snacks to be served to the airmen at dances and parties and for the Sunday morning breakfast.

Next was an enormous ballroom surrounded by small rooms, two music rooms where anyone interested in playing an instrument was allowed to practice, a studio where the French artist made posters and decorations for the club.

The artist, Monsierur Roulet was a heavy, bald man with small beady eyes and a big mouth that often smiled. He reminded Shannon of a butcher in his white apron spotted with red paint.

Mrs. Kline told her that the artist had been the dean of the art department at the University of Marseille before the war.

When they returned to the office, Shannon and Marcella shared a huge office with windows on all sides. In front of each window was a row of exotic plants that Mrs.

Klein had brought back from her various trips throughout the world.

Just outside their office was another small room with two desks for two French women, Annie, Mrs. Klein's private secretary, and Marie, the tour director. Both women smiled and welcomed Shannon.

Mrs. Klein gave Shannon a copy of the programs she was planning for the next month and asked her to make a list of ideas for decorations, entertainment and refreshments for each program. Shannon decided she would enjoy her work at the service club. She prepared activities for every day of the week from 9 am to 9 pm.

Because Shannon liked to sleep late in the morning and did not mind working late at night she chose to work from one in the afternoon to nine at night when the service club closed. Marcella worked from 9 am to one p.m.

One big surprise for Shannon was the way all the airmen seemed to fall in love with her at first sight. She had never imagined herself having so much attention from men. She had to admit she knew she was attractive and she had always been popular but to have hundreds of men showing interest in her was unexpected.

"The French women all seem so beautiful, so well dressed with great figures and lovely hair styles. Why do the airmen find us so desirable?"

"They're all homesick. We represent America to them so they all want to be with us."

That night there was another party. Shannon told Bobby she didn't think she'd be able to make it since she was tired.

"Oh, you have to make it," Bobby said. "You'll ruin our reputation as party girls. The service club women always show up. Why don't you take a nap and then get up and stop at the party for a drink."

After work Shannon took a refreshing nap. She was still sound asleep when Bobby and Marcella stopped by for her.

The same crowd was there and every one was already drunk. They were singing loud songs. No one was on key but no one cared.

Bobby joined in the singing. Marcella headed straight for the drinks. She came back with three glasses and Captain Rich who was carrying a bottle of Scotch.

"Have a drink, Shannon, so you can stand us," he said.

She drained her glass in one drink the way she had seen him do.

"Great, kid," he said, "You're learning." He filled the glass again.

"Van won't be here tonight," Bobby said, "so who's going to take his place and keep me entertained?"

Most of the men volunteered.

Bobby chose Maury, the youngest officer, known as the baby faced lieutenant.

"Come dance with me, Maury, so I won't be lonesome." Maury was beaming with happiness. Frank Sinatra was singing "In the Wee Small Hours" and Shannon wanted to listen but the people in the room were still singing off key.

When everyone seemed occupied, Shannon slipped out of the room and returned home to sleep. They were too drunk to know who was there and who wasn't. All they cared was that they were not alone.

Her room was at the far end of the hall, and her door was closed but she could still hear all the noise. She lay on her bed relaxing.

The next day Ellie told Shannon, "I'm renting an old mansion right outside of Evreux. Would you like to share it with me?"

Ellie warned Shannon, "Many years ago a man murdered his wife in that house and no one has lived there since. Everyone says her ghost roams the place but I don't believe in ghosts."

Shannon really liked Ellie but she did find the house a little frightening. There was a musty smell. All of the

furniture seemed to be at least one hundred years old. It had probably belonged to the murdered woman. It was all a deep maroon, dried blood red, faded navy blues, murky tans and hepatitis yellows. Every piece of wood was deformed with rococo figures of sterile flowers and stiff geometric forms.

The walls were covered with layers of dirty flowered wallpaper and every room had half a dozen pictures of land and seascapes painted by third rate 19th century artists.

One cold weekend in November Ellie had the weekend off from the hospital and she and Fred were going to the south of France. Shannon was home alone, in bed with the flu.

It was midnight and the old house was as quiet as a tomb. Shannon was feeling so lonely she got out of bed and let the canary out of her cage thinking she would be some kind of company. But she turned into a mad harpy attacking her with the force of the furies set on avenging some ancient crime. She fluttered around wildly pecking at Shannon's feet, her hands, her arms, her legs, not even leaving her face alone.

Shannon lay on the sofa in the living room, covered herself completely with a blanket and tried to fall asleep. But the bird landed on the blanket and kept picking at it. Finally Shannon got up and started chasing the bird around the room, determined to put her back in her cage. But she couldn't hold still for a moment, flew from room to room.

Shannon was feeling weak, sleepy and angry. After a while she gave up and lay back down and the canary began torturing her again.

In the end, Shannon opened the window and the canary flew out. She would either freeze or starve to death.

Shannon knew her roommate Ellie would be frantic when she learned her beloved canary was gone. Her fiancé Fred had given it to her saying he wanted to give her something golden.

Fred didn't want to give Ellie a ring because she wouldn't be able to wear it since they had to keep their engagement a secret. The Air Force had a rule that enlisted airmen and officers were not permitted to socialize and they would be punished if they did.

The fact that Ellie, a lieutenant, and Fred, an airman, were also of different races complicated matters. The racial situation on the base was ready to boil over and the base commander would have been only too happy to separate them by sending one to some far part of the world.

A storm was coming up. The wind was moaning outside her window and it was rattling a shutter in the back bedroom. She remembered the woman whose husband had murdered her in this house and the stories of her ghost hanging around here. Shannon had never believed in ghosts but lying there listening to the moaning wind and the pounding shutter she began to wonder if the dead woman was crying and complaining and trying to get back inside her house.

A rooster crowed even though it was the middle of the night. A group of dogs began barking. They had an ominous sound. She wondered if they were wolves. They didn't sound like ordinary dogs. There was something supernatural about them. They reminded her of the Roman dogs that guarded the gates of Hades.

Shannon thought she saw Ellie's canary at the window. She looked outside but it was only snow.

My roots are portable
My wings are flexed
On the road again
In the air
Can't land in Frankfurt
But can take off
And that's all I need
To do today.

Chapter Three
Portable Roots

When Ellie came home she hardly noticed that her beloved canary was missing. She and Fred had gone to the Riviera to get married and she was all excited as she described the ceremony to Shannon. "Since I'm still an officer and he's still an airman our marriage has to remain a secret. So I will continue living here and he will live in the barracks."

Shannon felt much better when she saw that Ellie was going to survive the loss of the bird. Ellie gave her some medicine and the next morning she felt well enough to go to work.

Like everyone else on the base Ellie took advantage of the untaxed liquor and she and Shannon usually had a night cap before going to bed. But this night Ellie drank Scotch and Shannon drank Nyquil.

Every night as Ellie drank her nightly Scotch she would lecture Shannon. "You have to watch this stuff,' she warned. "I enjoy drinking and I drink a lot but I know when to put the breaks on. There are more people than I care to count on this base who couldn't live a day without the bottle. They've let it get control of them. Use it but don't let it use you."

"Oh, I won't," Shannon said. And she almost kept her promise.

Ellie and Shannon became great friends. Whenever Ellie had a day off work if she was not with Fred, the two women would drive through the countryside in Ellie's Volkswagen, stopping every now and then to look at a castle or a church with lovely stained glass windows. They took sketch pads with them and drew pictures. Neither of them had any special talent as artists but they both enjoyed putting their impressions on paper and it helped them to appreciate the lovely scenery.

Ellie was working in the maternity ward. As they traveled, she would share her experiences with Shannon. "Those airmen's wives are something else. They keep screaming all the time, 'I hate my husband. That dirty bastard can never touch me again!' If they feel that way why do they get pregnant in the first place? But you should see how loving they are with their husbands once the baby arrives. Sometimes I wish I had a record to play for the husbands."

One Saturday morning Mrs. Kline told Shannon to remind all the airmen that there was going to be a big dance that evening. Some women were coming from Paris and there would be a live band. So all during the day Shannon went into the poolroom, the lounge where the men played cards, the table tennis room and the music rooms to remind the men of the dance.

The first hint Shannon had that something was wrong was when she told Cecil, a black airman, to come to the

dance. He had been practicing with a trumpet and was returning it to the check-out room.

Cecil looked at her, shocked. "Didn't they brief you?" he asked.

"What do you mean?' Shannon asked

'Don't you know the dances are for only half of the population?"

"I don't know what you're talking about."

"Don't put me on. Surely they told you the dances are only for the white airmen."

"I never heard of such a thing," Shannon said.

"I wish I could be here tonight," Cecil said, "I'd love to see how things go, but I have to be in Paris."

She went to Marcella's desk to ask her if what Cecil said was true.

"It shouldn't surprise you," Marcella said, "This base is as racist as Mississippi. There's not one black person on the base who hasn't been in jail at least once. I've been fighting with Mrs. Kline about this problem ever since I got here. You see, there's an old chaperone who comes with the French women and makes sure none of them dance with black airmen.

"At first the black airmen used to keep asking the women to dance. The women always said no. They had been warned if they danced with a black airmen they would not be allowed to return to the dances ever again. So now most of the black men do not come to the dances and the few who do just sit back and watch.

"It's a sad situation but I don't know what you and I can do about it. Mrs. Kline keeps saying that is the way Madame Nuit wants it and we can't go against her. I keep telling Mrs. Kline that Madame Nuit does not run the Service Club but Mrs. Kline says we need Madame Nuit to bring her women to the dances."

"I don't think I can put up with this situation," Shannon said.

"If you can think of a way to change things I'll be glad to help," Marcella said.

"Well, let's invite all the black airmen and if the French girls won't dance with them we will."

"Mrs. Kline will freak out," Marcella said, "But there's nothing I would like better. I'll make sure we have plenty of black airmen tonight."

Marcella and Shannon went into the artist's studio where he was painting some figures of women dressed in 1920 costumes during the Charleston.

"Look at these dancers," Marcella said proudly. I examined the line of dancing girls and was surprised and happy to find one beautiful black woman.

"I didn't want to make her black," the artist said, "I know Mrs. Kline won't like it but Miss Marcella insisted."

"She's beautiful," Shannon said.

He smiled proudly.

"Black people are good dancers," the artist said.

"I worked on another base where the head of the Service Club was from Mississippi," Marcella said, "Before our first dance she explained to all the Service Club workers that we could dance if we wanted to but if we did we could not refuse to dance with an airman because he was the wrong color or the wrong religion.

"She never danced because she did not want to dance with the black airmen. But I danced with everyone that asked me."

"That sounds fair enough," Shannon said.

"What isn't fair is Mrs. Kline's way. She insists we dance with the white airmen but never dance with the black airmen. At my first dance I danced with a black man and she told me never to do that again. It causes too much confusion."

"I think the rule about dancing with everyone or no one makes sense. I will tell Mrs. Kline that is my rule." Shannon said.

“”’Good luck,” Marcella said. “Mrs. Kline is very set in her ways.”

During the afternoon Marcella and Shannon decorated the ballroom so that it resembled a 1920 Chicago speakeasy. They set up tables with chairs around the edge of the floor and put the cardboard dancing girls on the stage.

Marcella and Shannon had prepared a floor show in which she was to sing several songs that were popular in the twenties and Shannon was to do a Charleston. The Diamonds, a group of black airmen were also a part of the show.

The ballroom started filling up early that evening. Mrs. Kline and Shannon were carrying refreshments into the ballroom.

“My, there are a lot of black airmen here tonight,” she said. “I wonder why. They don’t usually come to the dances.”

“I invited them,” Shannon said. You told me to remind all the airmen about the dance.”

“Oh, I should have told you we don’t encourage the black airmen because they sometimes make trouble.”

“What kind of trouble?’ Shannon asked.

“Well, the French girls don’t want to dance with them and sometimes they get upset and want to argue. You know how black men are.”

“I don’t know,” she said.

“Oh, they’re always fighting and causing trouble I hope they don’t start anything tonight.” She sat down the plate of chocolate chip cookies she had been carrying and returned to her office.

The French musicians arrived. The leader, Pierre, was a tall, jovial, baldheaded man about forty-five who spoke perfect English with a sensual French accent. Shannon explained to him that the theme of the dance was the 1920’s and he promised to play many 1920 tunes.

Both Marcella and Shannon wore Charleston outfits with short skirts, long blouses, small tight caps and lots of

beads. The men were used to seeing them in their air force uniforms and seemed delighted to see them in costumes.

"You ladies should dress that way all the time," Pierre said. "It looks much nicer than those old blue suits."

"I wish we could," Shannon said, "I hate uniforms."

Around seven-thirty the bus arrived with the French women and their chaperon, Madame Nuit. She was a tall, thin woman with many wrinkles around her mouth, none of them had come from laughter because she rarely even smiled. She always dressed in black and even wore black hose.

Shannon welcomed the women and led them into the kitchen where they stuffed themselves with spaghetti. Shannon wondered whether the women came to the dances for the food they bribed them with or because they wanted to meet American men.

When the women finished eating, Shannon ushered them into the ballroom. Madame Nuit walked next to her. "What are all the Black men during here?" she asked.

"They're airmen," Shannon said.

"But they don't usually come to the dances," Madame Nuit said, "Tell them to leave or I will take my girls out of here."

"We can't kick them out," Shannon said, "The Service Club belongs to them as much as it does to the white airmen."

"Go get Mrs. Kline. She'll know what to do."

"She's busy right now," Shannon said. "Sit down and relax. She will be here in a while."

Madame Nuit sat down, looking around the room, glowering at all the black airmen. In a few minutes she dragged herself out of the chair and crossed the room, stopping in front of each of "her" girls. "Don't let me catch any of you dancing with the black soldiers or I'll tell your families and I'll never bring you here again.: After she

made the rounds of all the girls she went back to her chair and sat there fanning herself.

Mrs. Kline came into the ballroom with Bob, the airman who drove the Motor Pool bus to pick up the French women, and Henry, an airman who spent a lot of time in the club running errands. She called Shannon and Marcella. "You girls should dance with Henry and Bob and get things started," she said. "I'm going to tell Pierre to start playing."

As Mrs. Kline walked towards Pierre, Madame Nuit shouted, "Mrs. Kline, get these black men out of here!"

Mrs. Kline tried to calm "Bye, Bye, Blackbird." Henry and Shannon began dancing. Bob and Marcella joined them on the floor.

Several black airmen stood up and walked towards the French girls. Madame Nuit jumped between them and the women.

Most of the women refused to dance with the men because they were afraid of Madame Nuit but a few defied her and started walking towards the center of the ballroom where some black men were waiting.

When they began dancing, Madame Nuit ran to them and started screaming, "I told you girls not to dance with the blacks! And I'll tell your bosses what whores you are! You will all lose your jobs!"

All of the women were frightened then. They apologized to the airmen and returned to their seats.

Satisfied that she'd done her duty for French womanhood, Madame Nuit hurried back to her seat and sat eagle like watching every moment her girls made.

Then Raymond, one of the Diamonds, the black group that was scheduled to sing, a short, handsome light skinned black man, marched up to a woman who was seated directly across the room from Madame Nuit and invited her to dance.

The girl accepted, assuming that he was white.

Madame Nuit could not make up her mind what his race was. She sat there examining him from afar, trying to decide.

She stared at them as they reached the dance floor. She kept bracing herself to get up and then sat back down. Finally she decided that he was black no matter how light his skin was and therefore not acceptable for her girls. She jumped up and stormed into the center of the dance floor.

"Black man, what are you doing dancing with one of my girls?"

He ignored Madame Nuit and kept dancing.

Madame Nuit snatched the woman from him. "And you, didn't I tell you about these black men? You can consider yourself without a job. I've given all of you my last warning. Tomorrow I speak to your boss."

"No!" the woman said, "I need my job. Please don't speak to my boss."

Madame Nuit twirled around and hurried to her seat.

The French girl returned to her chair in tears. She sat there for a few minutes and started out of the ballroom.

Shannon stopped her at the door. "Don't cry," she said.

"I didn't even know he was a black man," she said. "He was so light. And besides, I don't see what is wrong with dancing with a black man. They are just as nice as the white men."

"I don't see anything wrong with it either," Shannon said.

"She's going to tell my boss and I may lose my job. I need my job. My father is dead and I support the whole family. If I lose my job we have nothing to eat."

Shannon wrote her name and phone number on a piece of paper and handed it to the woman. "Let me know if you lose your job and I will call your boss and explain what really happened."

"Thank you so much," the woman said. "I feel better now. Let me give you my name and phone number too. Her name was Rene and she lived in the country near Evreux.

Then two of the Diamonds asked Shannon and Marcella to dance. Without a pause they both accepted. As

the four of them started towards the dance floor, Madame Nuit jumped out of her seat and ran around the ballroom frantically searching for Mrs. Kline.

In the meantime Shannon and Marcella danced with their black partners.

Mrs. Kline came out of her office. She was trying to calm Madame Nuit who was insisting loudly that Mrs. Kline make her girls stop dancing.

Mrs. Kline was trying to avoid trouble. She waited until the music ended and then she asked Shannon and Marcella to come into the office with her for a few minutes.

Mrs. Kline was trying to appear calm. She forced a smile on her lips but her eyes looked frightened.

Mrs. Kline's secretary was seated at Mrs. Kline's desk going over some letters she was going to type.

"Annie, why don't you go into the ballroom and dance a little?" Mrs. Kline told her.

Annie smiled and obligingly left the room.

Mrs. Kline closed the door.

"I don't know what we are going to do with Madame Nuit," she said. "She is so emotional. She came running into the office shouting,"Mrs.Kline! Oh, Mrs. Kline! Come quick and see what your girls are doing. She was so hysterical I thought you two must be on stage doing a strip tease. She was like a mad woman.

"I followed her into the ballroom and she kept insisting I should make you girls stop dancing with the black airmen. The only way I could calm her down was to promise I would tell you not to do it again. So I'm asking both of you, please help me. I don't want trouble in my service club. This is my home, what I live for. I can't bear to have trouble." She looked as if she might burst into tears at any moment.

Shannon felt sorry for her but she remembered that the black airmen had feelings too. "Madame Nuit does not run the Service Club," she said. "You shouldn't allow her to tell you how to run it."

"Please don't start that argument now, "Mrs. Kline begged. 'We've been through this before and I've tried to explain the situation. We have a hard time getting girls for our dances. Madame Nuit is known to these girls' families and respected. The girls are permitted to come only because she chaperones them. If we want the dances to continue we must keep Madame Nuit happy."

"I'd rather have no dances than have dances restricted to white airmen, "Marcella said.

"I feel the same way," Shannon said. "The Service Club is supposed to be for all the airmen. We can't allow the French women to say which airmen can use the club."

"Please try to understand," Mrs. Kline said, "The dances mean a great deal to the boys. They look forward to them. They are always asking me when is the next dance. We can't let them down. They're so far from home. These dances are one of the few real pleasures they have."

"But that's true for the black airmen as well as the whites," Shannon said.

"I know it is," Mrs. Kline said sadly. "If only there was something we could do about it. I'd like to see all my boys happy. I wish we could bring in some black women. It breaks my heart to have things the way they are."

"We have to change things," Marcella said.

"Don't you think I've tried?' Mrs. Kline said. "For a while the black boys were really giving us problems. They complained to the base commander. They even threatened to write their congressmen or the president. The base commander said if we didn't solve the problem we would have to stop having dances.

"Sergeant Robbins, the black boy who sometimes helps us out in the service club spoke with the black airmen and explained that the pleasures they do have such as the music room where they practice their jazz any time they wish, the pool tables, the whole club might close down if they did not stop complaining and finally they stopped.

"I can't understand why it all started up again. But I'm counting on your girls to help me keep things calm."

"Let's go back now and get the boys dancing. Now don't you girls do anything to upset Madame Nuit."

"Are you ordering us not to dance with the black men?" Marcella asked.

"I'm begging you not to" Mrs. Kline said, close to tears.

"I'm sorry, Mrs. Kline," Shannon said, "If I can't dance with the black men I can't dance with any of them."

"But you have to dance. That is our job. There's only about 30 women here and 500 airmen. We'd better get out there."

"Which do you prefer, are we to dance with everyone or no one?" Marcella asked.

"We'll talk about it later."

As soon as they entered the ballroom, Madame Nuit came running up to Mrs. Kline, "Look! Look!" She pointed to Mrs. Kline's secretary Annie who was dancing with a black airman.

"I'm ready to take my girls home right now," Madame Nuit shouted. "I can't have them exposed to such examples. If you can't keep your people acting decently I will not allow my girls to come back. Their parents put them in my hands because they know they can trust me to see that they are well behaved."

"Just a minute," Mrs. Kline said, "I spoke with the two girls who danced earlier but I did not get a chance to speak with Annie. I'll speak with her as soon as the song ends."

"If any more of your people dance with the blacks I am taking my girls and we will never come back!" She was shouting so loudly that everyone in the ballroom turned to look at her.

The music ended and Mrs. Kline ran up to Annie. "Annie, how could you do this to me? You know the problems we have had with the black airmen!"

"Oh, Mrs. Kline, I'm so sorry. You know I don't like dancing with those black men. I'm not used to it and they frighten me. But Elmer is such a nice boy and he asked me to dance and I didn't want to hurt him. I wanted to say no but I just couldn't." She started to cry.

"It's my fault for sending you out to dance," Mrs. Kline said, putting her arm around Annie. "I should have known one of them would ask you to dance. They are out to cause trouble tonight."

Annie went back into the office.

Only a few couples were dancing now. Everyone seemed upset by the happenings of the evening.

"Marcella, why don't you and Shannon ask Henry and Bob to dance? If the others see you dancing they will dance also."

"I'd rather not dance," Marcella said.

"You have to dance," Mrs. Kline said.

The two couples danced and then the band decided to have an intermission. Marcella and Shannon made final preparations for the floor show.

The Diamonds, the black singing group, told Shannon and Marcella, "We're only singing for you two. We feel stupid entertaining at a dance where our people are mistreated."

Marcella introduced the Diamonds. She said, "We are very fortunate to have some fellows with us tonight who are like birds. They sing for those who deserve their songs and for those who don't. Here they are the Diamonds!"

There was wild applause as the five Diamonds walked on stage wearing identical black suits with white shirts and black ties.

They sang "Five Foot Two, Eyes of Blue," "Ain't she sweet," and "Bye, Bye, Blackbird."

For an encore, they sang "If I had a Hammer."

Giovane Mazzola, an Italian American who had once been a professional dancer did the Charleston with Shannon, dancing to "The Charleston" and "Sweet Georgia Brown."

The audience wanted an encore so they repeated one of the dances since they had not had time to practice a third dance.

Marcella sang "The Gypsy in my soul," "Blues in the Night," and "My Funny Valentine."

Then Mrs. Kline announced, "Thank you all for coming to our monthly dance. Get home safely, girls. Good night, everyone. Hope you all enjoyed a night in the 1920's."

That night Shannon told her black roommate Ellie all about the racism in the service club.

"It doesn't surprise me at all," Ellie said. "I think racism is the real reason that Frank and I can't be open about our marriage. They say we can't date because I am an officer and he is an airman but I think the race question is why they will not make an exception for us."

Freedom's just another word
What's in a word?
Give me liberty or give me
Nothing left to lose
I pledge my troth
To all my beliefs
With liberty and justice for all
who can afford them
And give us
All the freedom
Money can buy

Chapter Four
All The Freedom Money can buy

The next day Shannon entered the empty ballroom. She sat in a chair and looked around the room.

"Well, little lady, you've stirred up quite a brew."

She gasped. She had thought she was alone.

It was Sergeant Robbins, the black airman who worked a few hours in the service club, the man who, according to Mrs. Kline, had helped her solve the black problem. He was a good looking light skinned black man, about 35. He was usually quiet. Whenever Shannon had noticed him he was doing some errand for Mrs. Kline or sitting alone reading a book.

Shannon was eager to hear what he had to say now.

"What do you mean?" she asked.

"You know what I'm talking about," he said. "Why did you want to get those fellows all upset again? Don't you realize that you are only hurting them and yourself?"

"I just want to see that their rights are respected," she said. 'The service club belongs to them as much as it belongs to the white airmen."

"You've got a lot to learn about life," he said, smoking his pipe. "It should belong to them as much as to the white airmen perhaps. But it doesn't. You're too idealistic, always thinking in terms of theory never in terms of practice.

"The service club, like everything American, is owned by the white power structure and it's their right to say how it is used. If we owned it, we could make the rules. You'd better learn the facts of life before you really get yourself messed up and all those fellows with you. Didn't you realize that all those men had come to accept things the way they are? You should never have promised something that isn't yours to give."

"Do you disapprove of people fighting for what is rightfully theirs?" she asked.

"No, but I disapprove of people sticking their nose in where they don't belong even if their nose is as lovely as your little turned up Irish nose."

"Are you saying there's no place for whites in the black people's struggle for their rights?"

"That's exactly what I believe," he said, blowing smoke from his pipe. "I think the best thing whites can do for blacks is leave them alone and let them decide what they need to do."

"As long as blacks and whites both live in America, their problems are shared."

"I'd like to see all blacks living together in our own country. In addition, I do not care what happens in the service club. I work here because I can use the little pay they give me. But I never get involved in white folks' business.

Well, I enjoyed our talk. See if you can't stay out of trouble, young lady." He left the club.

Shannon was confused. She had thought she was doing the right thing trying to integrate the club. Was it possible Sergeant Robbins was right?"

When she saw Mrs. Kline, Shannon said, "I worried all night about the dance. Isn't there some way we could get another chaperone? I am sure it's against Air Force polity to have such a racist on the base."

Mrs. Kline blushed. "It has nothing to do with Air Force policy.

"I've tried to get another chaperone but Madame Nuit is the only one the girls' mothers will trust. She's known and respected. All we can do is keep things as quiet as possible. I spoke with Sergeant Robbins and he promised to ask the black airmen not to come to the next dance. So you girls must not encourage any of them to attend the dance."

That afternoon Cliff Jones, a red haired airman from Tennessee told Shannon, "I was really disappointed at the dance the other night." She thought he was going to complain that there were so many black men there. Instead he said, "It's a shame we can't get some black women to come and dance with the black airmen. After all they are in the Air Force too."

One night Marcella had a Jam Session. She invited all the singers and musicians on the base to perform. The Diamonds sang and a black jazz band, The Night Riaders played. Marcella sang and Shannon did a modern dance. A white jazz band, led by an officer, Colonel Ben had a singer with lovely red hair and a great figure. Her name was Regina and her voice was captivating. She was the wife of an airman stationed on the base.

The show went over very well. Mrs. Kline was a little upset when she learned that an officer had taken part in an enlisted men's show. "I only hope Captain Frydel doesn't hear about it," she said, "He doesn't even want officers coming into the service club, let alone taking part in the programs. You should be more careful, Marcella."

"I'm sorry, Mrs. Kline. But the boys enjoyed it and I don't see any harm done."

"Let's hope not," she said, "and in the future please be more careful."

When the club closed for the night, Marcella invited everyone who had taken part in the show to come to her room for a drink. "It's just a little something to show my appreciation for the help you all gave me."

It was the smallest party Shannon had attended on the base but it was by far the most enjoyable. There was room to dance, time to get to know one another and the music was soft enough to allow everyone to think and talk a little.

Marcella had repainted her room to get rid of that awful olive green seen everywhere on the base. Hers was the only blue room in the building and she had decorated it in black, silver and blue. It afforded the perfect atmosphere for such a get-to-gether.

She had prepared small appetizers and a wide selection of drinks. She had a lovely hi-fi set and a great collection of records.

Everyone drank a little but no one got drunk, not even Colonel Ben. He seemed to have taken a great interest in Regina.

"We should have invited Mrs. Kline," Raymond, one of the black singers, said as he danced with Marcella.

"And Madame Nuit," added Mike, the black drummer who was dancing with Shannon.

Everyone laughed.

Around one a.m., Regina said she had to go home.

"The night is young," Marcella said.

"Not for me," Regina said, "If I don't go soon my husband and daughter will come looking for me."

"I'll drive you home," Ben said.

"Do you think you should?" she asked.

"Of course I should," he said. "It's too late for you to be out on the base alone."

They said goodnight and left. Everyone else stayed until four a.m.

The next morning both Marcella and Shannon had to be at work at 9 a.m. They were both half asleep as they walked across the base to the service club.

"I'm glad Mrs. Kline doesn't come to work until one today," Marcella said. "I'm too tired to face her this morning."

But when they walked into the service club, Mrs. Kline was waiting for them. Captain Frydel was with her.

"Come in, girls," Mrs. Kline said. "Sit down. Captain Frydel would like to speak to you."

Captain Frydel took a deep breathe. "First of all, I have to remind you that the base is like a small town. It is impossible to keep secrets here. Gossip travels faster than light. And second, I want to make the point that the vast majority of the population here is masculine. Therefore you girls as part of the small feminine minority are going to be a focus point. Your every movement is watched and noted.

"And since you're working in the service club the boys come to think of you as though you were their sisters. They look up to you and they expect you to behave like saints, in the way boys always want their sisters to act.

"Now I realize you're civilians and the Air Force has no control over your private lives. But under the circumstances I believe we do have the right, in fact the obligation to call certain facts to your attention. For instance, although you are civilians, we give you officers' status which entitles you to live in the officers' headquarters and to use the officers' club. In return we ask you to obey the same rule the officers are required to obey: You are not to mix socially with enlisted men.

"Well, it has been brought to our attention at Special Services on quite a few separate occasions that both of you are socializing with airmen."

"I wish you'd be more specific," Marcella said. "I don't understand exactly what you mean by socializing. Several times on my way to work I have given airmen rides in my car to the service club. Could that be called socializing?"

Mrs. Kline looked at Captain Frydel questioningly.

"It could be," he said, "if it gave the other airmen something to talk about."

"Oh, I get you now," Marcella said,' You're not really concerned with whether or not we socialize with airmen. What you're upset about is the fact that we might "socialize" as you call it with black airmen. Why didn't you say so in the beginning?"

"Please don't go bringing race into this," Captain Frydel said. "All I was trying to do was remind you of the fact that you girls have officers' status and as such are not permitted to mingle socially with enlisted men be they white or black.

"I realize it's difficult for you to work with airmen all day under 'social conditions' and then sudden cease all social relationships with them when your work day ends. But that is exactly what I'm asking you to do.

"And since you mention the fact that some of your airmen friends are black, let me remind you that just as women are in the minority on this base and therefore in the spot light as you might say, Blacks are also in the minority and therefore more noticeable.

"What I'm trying to say is every time you girls socialize with a black airman you can count on the news traveling all over the base."

"So what you're saying now is we're not to have anything to do with black airmen. Is that it?" Marcella asked.

Captain Frydel was becoming angry. "Don't you tell me what I'm saying! Just listen to me. Allow me to finish. As you know there are many southern airmen on the base and they all have the idea that any white girl who befriends a

black man is shall I say 'a loose woman' that is a woman of poor morals. Now, it's very important that the airmen respect you service club workers. Therefore, you have to bear in mind the boys' personal feelings."

Shannon was getting angry also. "And we have to consider their prejudices?" she asked.

"If necessary," he said. "I certainly don't mean you have to share their prejudices. But you do have to consider them. And keep them in mind when deciding your personal conduct. And let me warn you, once your reputation is ruined you are no longer able to perform your function in the service club. I've had to let several girls go because their reputations were blemished. Mrs. Kline can tell you that."

"That's right," Mrs. Kline said. "Why I remember one girl who came to us pregnant. Of course we didn't know it when we hired her. But as soon as we found out about it we had to let her go."

Captain Frydel laughed. "What Mrs. Kline is saying is we don't want you girls getting pregnant. Well, I think we can trust you girls not to get yourselves pregnant. All I'm worried about is that you keep your reputations clean which entails even more than keeping your actions clean. For as you well know innocent actions can lead to a bad reputation."

"So we're not to speak to black airmen when we are off work?" Shannon asked.

"That's silly, "Mrs. Kline said. "We have to be friendly to all the boys. Otherwise they won't want to come to the club."

"You can speak to all the airmen," the captain said. "but you don't need to carry on long conversations. Don't put them in your car. Be friendly to all of them. Wave, say hello and be on your way."

"Sometimes that's difficult to do," Mrs. Kline said, "The boys want to know what programs we are planning and things like that. Talking to the airmen is one of our most valuable ways of advertising our programs."

"You may have to find new ways," Captain Frydel said. "We can't take risks where the girls' reputations are involved."

"Surely you can understand what Captain Frydel means," Marcella said.

"We can go on telling the white airmen about our programs. He's only concerned with our being seen talking to black airmen."

"Well, maybe he's right," Mrs. Kline said, "as long as there's no problem about telling the white airmen about our programs."

The captain turned to Marcella. "I asked you once before to stop putting words into my mouth, Miss Morgan. "If I need your help as an interpreter I'll ask for it. I meant exactly what I said. I don't think you girls should carry on any conversation with any airman outside of the service club."

"I don't think it would hurt anything if they only spoke with white airmen," Mrs. Kline said.

"You all heard what I said," Captain Frydel continued. "I don't care if every airman stops using the club. I will not have you girls ruining your reputations. Then I would definitely have to close down the club."

"We'd better do as Captain Frydel says," Mrs. Kline said, concerned.

"There's one last point, I'd like to make before I leave you," the captain said. "That is the fact that no officers are to be allowed to enter the club at any time unless they are on official business."

He lowered his voice. "It has been brought to my attention that a certain officer took part in a service club program last night, such a thing is not to happen again. I hope I can count on all of you to see that our rule of no fraternization is strictly enforced.

"Remember our office receives regular reports on the service club. Every time something happens that an airman

doesn't like he comes to us. So please help us to protect the reputation of the service club."

He picked up his magazine. "I guess that's all I had to say, girls. And if you have any problems feel free to come to me." He shook every woman's hand and left.

"Captain Frydel doesn't really understand how a service club runs," Mrs. Kline said. "We need to talk to the airmen on our way to work. That's how we publicize our programs. But I guess we'd better go along with him." She signed resignedly.

Then Mrs. Kline gathered the two girls close to her. "Captain Frydel was so worried about our having that officer here last night because he's involved in a nasty little scandal. The worse part of it is the fact that we had the girl here too. You see, Colonel Ben and that red headed singer are involved with each other and most of the people on the base know all about it. Colonel Ben's wife already left him and the singer's husband who is a sergeant is threatening to divorce her and keep their little girl. It's a bad business and we have to see that the service club doesn't get involved. That's why I was so disturbed yesterday when I saw them here. If you had only asked me about it in advance, Marcella, I could have warned you. Well, it's over now as far as we're concerned. Let's just see that they never come back here."

Mrs. Kline went into the check out room then and Marcella whispered, "I'm about ready to leave this place. I refuse to work where they try to run my private life."

"I've been ready to leave since the day I arrived, "Shannon said.

"Oh, I have too," Marcella said. "But this morning was the final blow. I am definitely going to ask for a transfer."

"I think I'll just go on living as I please and wait for them to kick me out."

"I don't want kicked out," Marcella said, "Then I'd have to make a decision as to where to go and what to do with my life. I'll ask for a transfer and the first opening that comes up will determine my future. I've made too many decisions lately and came to regret most of them."

A few days later, Shannon was alone in the office when Regina came in looking for Marcella. Regina was wearing a white sheath and white shoes and looked beautiful.

Regina was very disappointed to learn that Marcella was not in.

"I really need to talk to her," she said. "I've had a terrible day. Is it okay if I just sit and wait for her?"

"Of course," Shannon said, pulling a chair around beside her desk.

"You know Colonel Ben and I are seeing each other," she said softly. "Well, we love each other very much but we have so many problems. The base is transferring him to Spain. He wants me to get a divorce and meet him in Spain.

But I can't leave my little daughter. My husband would never let me have her.

"It wouldn't be so hard on me if her father wanted her because he loved her. However, it is not that. He wants her to punish me. He knows that my daughter and I are crazy about each other. I cannot even be sure he would be good to her. He might try to punish her too. Just because she loves me so much. And in any case he would try to get her to hate me. I'm so mixed up.

"My husband says he still loves me and wants me to stay with him and Kathy. But if he really loved me he couldn't stand to see me so unhappy. If only I could take Kathy with me. She and Ben get along very well. We could be so happy together. How do people get their lives so messed up?"

Shannon felt sorry for her but she couldn't think of any way to help her.

"If only I had met Ben before I met Tom. Sometimes I feel I'm out of tune with my life and this is my punishment. What would you do in my place?"

'I don't know," Shannon said. "I'd probably be as mixed up as you are."

Marcella came into the club. "Hello, Regina," she said. "What are you doing here?"

"I'm crying on Shannon's shoulder. She was kind enough to offer it and I desperately needed a listener."

"Is it the same problem?" Marcella asked.

"The same. Only worse. Ben is being transferred. Oh, God, Marcella, what will I do without him?"

"I'm certainly not the one to come to for advice," Marcella said. "My own marriage lasted exactly one month and four days. Now that's not any kind of preparation for a marriage counselor."

"How did you live through it?"

"Live through it? I'm not through it yet. I've goofed up my own life. I want no part in goofing up any one else's life."

She brushed her hair out of her eyes. "When I was nineteen years old I did a very stupid thing. I married a junkie. He was a musician in the band I was singing with. He was handsome and seemed like a nice guy. I didn't know he was on drugs. But I probably would have married him anyway. I was so ignorant.

"We started arguing the first night and he hit me. He hit me almost every day after that and finally I got enough sense and I left him. I got a divorce but I'm a Catholic and as far as the church is concerned we're still married so I have to be careful not to fall in love with anyone else."

"I'm sorry," Regina said.

"I'm not really a good Catholic but I don't want to be forced to give up my religion. It's all I have left. How did we get on such a morbid subject?"

"It's my fault," Regina said. "I seem to be living a morbid life. But let's cheer up. Does anyone know any good jokes?"

"I know lots of jokes," Marcella said, "but I always forget the last line so I'd better forget them."

"Well, I'm gonna go home and have a good cry," Regina said and she left the office.

The next month there was another dance. Marcella and Shannon begged Mrs. Kline to get another chaperone but she insisted it was impossible to find someone the French girls' parents would trust.

Shannon and Marcella were careful not to encourage any of the black airmen to come to the dance because Mrs. Kline had told them Madame Nuit warned her that this was the last dance with the French girls if there was any interracial dancing.

On the night of the dance both Marcella and Shannon were depressed. They went through the motions of preparing for the dance without really caring how it turned out.

Madame Nuit entered the club first. "I hope those blacks aren't here tonight," she said, her face set in a deep from.

Shannon ignored her. "You can put your coats in this room," she said, leading the women into one of the music rooms.

Shannon was pleased to see that Rene was still with them.

"How are you?" Shannon asked her.

"I'm fine," Rene said. "I didn't lose my job but I must be very careful tonight because she won't give me another chance."

The band began playing. "Why don't you two girls get a partner and begin dancing?" Mrs. Kline asked.

"We've decided it is best if we don't dance tonight," Marcella said.

"Maybe you're right," Mrs. Kline said, sadly shaking her head.

There were only a few black airmen in the room. Several of them asked the French women to dance. Madame Nuit jumped up but the women politely refused and remained seated.

Shannon saw Sergeant Robbins sitting in a dark corner, alone. She joined him.

"I see you've finally learned your lesson, he said. "I am glad to see you are a fast learner."

"I haven't given up" Shannon said," I'm still determined to get rid of Madame Nuit."

"Madame Nuit was here before you came and she'll be here long after you go. Don't waste your energy on her. "

The dance dragged on without one black airman having danced. Madame Kline sat surveying the scene like a queen who had just been restored to her throne and whose powers had been multiplied with the restoration.

Shannon wished she could walk up to that awful woman and slap that nasty smirk from her ugly face.

Before the evening ended, Raymond, one of the Diamonds, removed her smirk with much more gusto than Shannon could ever have managed. He walked into the ballroom like a king, his head high, his walk dignified and on his arm was one of the most beautiful women Shannon had ever seen.

They walked right into the center of the ballroom, directly in front of Madame Nuit and began to dance. Raymond held her so close it looked like she must have had difficulty breathing.

Madame Nuit definitely had trouble breathing. She kept gasping and sighing and clinging to the sides of her chair. She looked around the room for Mrs. Kline who had seen the couple arriving and ran into her office to avoid a confrontation.

Shannon looked around the room at the black airmen. They were all beaming. It was as if they were dancing with

that beautiful girl in front of Madame Nuit. It was a personal victory for each of them. It certainly was a victory for Shannon. That one incident had saved the night.

After the dance ended, Mrs. Kline appeared and asked our hero not to bring the girl into the club again.

"Is that an order?" Raymond asked. "or just a request? Because if it is a request I will forget it but if it is an order I will complain to Captain Frydel, the base commander and the President of the United States, my commander in chief.

"I shall notify each of them that until the service club supplies me with a dancing partner I shall continue to bring my own girl. Now will you answer my question, was it an order of a request?"

Mrs. Kline looked frighten. "Don't you dare threaten me," she said.

"I'm not threatening you," he said calmly. "I'm merely informing you where I stand. Now do I have your permission to bring my girl to the service club dances or do I have to write the base commander for his permission?"

"Why must you fellows always cause trouble?" Mrs. Kline asked.

"You didn't answer my question, Mrs Kline, is my girl welcome in the club?"

"Bring her," Mrs. Kline said, shaking her head in disbelief.

Ellie laughed when Shannon told her about Raymond and his French girlfriend and the way they had integrated the service club.

**A circle has no end.
It does not begin.
It goes on and on
Into eternity
Or infinity
Which ever
Is longer.**

Chapter Five
Circles

On Monday afternoon Regina brought her daughter Kathy into the service club. Kathy was a lovely little girl with long reddish blond hair. She was seven years old and wore a blue dress that brought out the blue of her big eyes.

"Kathy, I want you to meet my friends, Shannon and Marcella."

"I'm glad to meet you," Kathy said. Then she couldn't hold back her enthusiasm any longer and she shouted, "Look what my mommy bought me!" She held up a beautiful doll that was almost as big as she was.

But her joy vanished when she remembered the occasion for the gift. She had tears down her face as she said, "Mommy says I can hold my baby doll on the long nights when she is gone."

Kathy ran to her mother. "But I will still miss you, Mommy. Why can't I go with you? Please take me with you."

"Stop, darling, or you will make me cry. I have already explained why you can't come with me. Someone has to stay and take care of Daddy. You will do that for me, won't you, sweetheart?"

"I don't want to take care of Daddy. I want to go with you."

Regina put her arms around her daughter. "I love you so much, Kathy and your Daddy loves you."

Regina turned to Marcella and Shannon, "Well, the decision has been made. For better or for worse. Ben leaves tonight for Spain. And I'm going to Iowa to stay with his family until Tom and I get our divorce and Ben and Alice get theirs. Then I'm going to Spain to marry Ben. And my darling Kathy is going to stay with her Daddy Tom like a good little girl, aren't you, sweetheart?"

Kathy shook her head, "Yes" Tears ran down her face.

"I'm leaving tomorrow morning for the states," Regina said. "I just wanted to tell you ladies goodbye and to introduce you to my precious daughter so you will see how much I'm giving up. It's an awful price to pay. I'm paying for my love."

"What do you mean, Mommy?" Kathy asked.

"I'm just telling the women how much I love you."

"Then take me with you."

"We'd better get home now," Regina said.

She kissed Marcella and Shannon on the cheeks and promised to write to them.

"Oh, let me give you Ben's address before I go. Write to him. He will be so lonely in Spain. All his friends are here. It's hard on him too."

The two women took Ben's address and promised to write.

"Goodbye, "Kathy said. "It was nice knowing you." She took her mother's hand and they walked away.

There was great news the next day. "Guess what," Marcella said, 'Mrs. Kline finally got rid of Madame Nuit. We have a new chaperone!"

Mrs. Kline verified the news, "Girls, we have solved the dance problem. Madame Nuit is not coming anymore. Her niece will be the new chaperone. She's much younger and easier to get along with."

"Anyone is easier to get along with than Madame Nuit," Marcella said.

The two women spread the news throughout the service club. All of the airmen were happy to be free of the "Old Mean Vulture."

When Saturday night came, the ballroom filled early. Mrs. Kline scampered around making sure everything would be ready when the French women arrived. "It's a shame so many black airmen have to be here on that girl's first night," she complained. "I do hope there's no trouble."

It was a crisp November night and there was a touch of excitement in the air. The wicked witch had been conquered and the crowd was gathered to enjoy the spoils.

When the huge old bus pulled up in front of the service club, Shannon went outside to greet the women.

For a minute she expected to see Madame Nuit climbing out of the bus.

Several airmen had gathered around to catch a glimpse of the new chaperone. She was a tall, thin young woman about thirty years old. Her black hair was curled softly around her face but there was something hard and determined about her expression. She had the same beak nose and glaring eyes as her aunt, Madame Nuit. But her smile was friendly and reassuring.

"I'm Yvonne Nuit," she said, giving Shannon her gloved hand.

"I'm Shannon Owens. It's nice to meet you. So happy you could accompany the women."

Shannon led Yvonne and the French women into the music room so they could hang up their coats on a hall tree. The coats that did not fit on the tray were put on top of the piano.

Marcella and Shannon had fixed a large table full of various sandwiches and cookies. Marcella brought in a large pot of steaming hot coffee.

Shannon introduced Marcella and Yvonne, then left the two of them talking as she went to greet Rene, the woman who had been so frightened of losing her job. She was sitting on a chair next to the piano. She smiled when she saw Shannon.

"How's everything with you?" Shannon asked.

"I'm feeling well," Rene said.

After the women finished eating, they went into the ballroom.

Pierre, the bandleader was in the ballroom. Shannon welcomed him.

"I see you got rid of the curse," he said, laughing. "Congratulations. We'll play some special tunes to celebrate." The band began to play and many airmen started towards the French women. There were many black airmen among them.

Yvonne Nuit, the new chaperone did not bat an eye. She was happily talking to an airman who was sitting next to her.

But once more the French women refused to dance with a black man and the dance began with only white dancers on the floor.

Later, when there was no one else near them, Rene told Shannon that Yvonne had given strict orders no one was to dance witth a black man. If anyone did, she would not say a word to them during the dance but they could be sure they would never be allowed to come to another dance and their families and bosses would be notified.

"I can't understand why they hate the blacks so much," Rene said. "It hurts me to have to refuse to dance with them. It's even worse now that Madame Nuit is gone. Before the black airmen knew why we couldn't dance with them. Now they believe it's because we ourselves don't want to. Many of

us would be happy to dance with them if we were allowed to."

Shannon was so angry she didn't know what to do. What they thought was a victory was a great defeat. Yvonne was much more subtle than her aunt and therefore more difficult to fight.

When Shannon told Marcella about her conversation with Rene, Marcella said, "That's just what I thought. I didn't think all of the women would refuse to dance without orders. Well what do we do now?"

"You and I dance with the black airmen and the French girls dance with the white airmen."

But all of the black airmen were brooding and not one of them asked Marcella or Shannon to dance.

Shannon sat down next to Sergeant Robbins. "So you got rid of Madame Nuit," he said.

"Yes," I said, "but her replacement is even worse."

"Naturally, Sergeant Robbins said. "You kill one dragon and a stronger one rises from its roots."

"We'll think of something," Shannon said.

"Don't think," he said, "Things are bad enough now. Don't go making them worse."

"You are so pessimistic," she said. "Why can't you ever be optimistic?"

"I am a realist," he said.

Shannon stood in the corner near the punch bowl and watched the white airmen and their partners dancing as the black airman sat around disappointed.

Everyone had come to the dance expecting things to be different and they were being served the same old rancid meat in a brand new platter.

"It's a shame Raymond isn't here with his girl," Shannon thought.

His appearance at the last dance had won a moral victory.

She made a mental note to remind him to come to the next dance.

And maybe his girl could bring some friends.

When the band began the last dance of the evening Cecil, a black airman, asked Shannon to dance. Grateful for the opportunity to upset the racist apple cart, she accepted.

As they danced, Yvonne Nuit appeared to be completely caught up in a conversation with a French girl sitting next to her. They were both laughing.

But once the dance ended and Yvonne and the French girls left the club, Mrs. Kline called Shannon and Marcella. "Yvonne Nuit feels it is best if you two girls don't dance at all. I guess she's got a point. It stirs up the airmen when you girls dance. We certainly don't want any trouble."

That settled it. Shannon was going to make certain that Raymond and his girl attended the next dance, with friends if possible.

Winter was rapidly taking control of the base, touching every tree, every blade of grass, every building with her icy fingers and smothering every souvenir of summer's laughing face and autumn's rainbows.

Suddenly one morning, all the leaves had fallen and the trees stood bare like thousands of slender nudes exposed to the winds that came more frequently now to bring the sighs of the dead under every door.

Shannon had always felt closer to death in the winter. Her mind started wandering down dark solitary paths seeking fresh graves and deserted cemeteries. This year, being on a dreary air base where she felt lonely much of the time, Shannon found herself in a deep depression.

She saw it was going to be a long cold winter and she would have to conserve all her strength if she was to have a new surge of life come spring.

It was a long cold winter but the first of December finally arrived and life lightened up as everyone made plans for Christmas.

Before Shannon could begin making plans for the holidays she received a phone call from her sister Jeanette in

Ohio. "I'm getting married December 30th and I want you to come home and be my bride's maid."

Shannon had not been home for two years and she really missed her family. She had always been close to Jeanette and she did not want to miss her wedding so she got permission to take her vacation now.

Although it was a bitter cold day with a pale gray sky the sun was strong. As usual the wind was loud and powerful. It centered in the pines behind the service club and on the road to Evruex making weird melancholy ghostly music.

When Shannon reached the club, Mrs. Kline and Marcella were busy planning Christmas programs and making lists of decorations and items they would be needing.

The service club was open every day of the week and on all holidays so the women had to decide which holidays they wanted to work and which one holiday they would like to be free.

Mrs. Kline had taken Halloween off. Marcella had joked, saying "It is the perfect holiday for that old witch." Mrs. Kline considered the club her home and insisted on working for all the big important holidays, which was fine with the other workers.

Marcella wanted New Year's Eve off because she had become good friends with the Base Commander's young wife and was invited to a big party at the Base Commander's home.

Shannon explained that she wanted Christmas off and the last two weeks of December so she could attend her sister's wedding.

Mrs. Kline was in her glory as she poured herself into making the service club Christmasy for the boys. She sent Shannon and Sergeant Robbins to choose a Christmas tree. "Make sure it's nice and fresh and green and fluffy," she said. "and tall enough to touch the ceiling. Sergeant Robbins has the measurements. I'm counting on the two of you." She patted Shannon on the arm.

"This is the first year that I have not chosen the tree myself," she said confidentially. "Shannon, you are the first girl I ever had that I could really depend on. So I need you to do it this year. I'm so busy and besides I won't always be here. I want to make sure there's someone I can trust to take over when I am gone."

Shannon had a strange feeling that Mrs. Kline was testing her so that she could feel free to die. She knew dying was the only way Mrs. Kline would ever leave the service club and her precious boys.

"Mrs. Kline sure thinks a lot of you," Sergeant Robbins said when they were in the big truck on the way to pick up the tree.

"I really don't know why," she said. "I guess it's because she doesn't really know me. We are so different."

"Not really," Sergeant Robbins said. "You two have a lot in common. You are both trying to make the service club as homey as possible for the airmen. You just don't agree on what homey is."

"I don't agree with you," Shannon said. "The service club is the center of Mrs. Kline's world. She hates to leave it at night and can't wait to arrive each morning. Myself, I hate the place. I dread going to work and can't wait to escape each night."

"That's just because you haven't succeeded in making the club the way you would like it to be," he said, slowly drawing on his pipe. "I have watched the way you put your heart into those dances.

Mrs. Kline could not care anymore about the club than you do."

Shannon sighed. "You never seem to understand me."

"I think I understand you better than you understand yourself."

They drove to a large clearing at the edge of the base. The ground was covered with fresh cut pines and firs of all sizes and shapes.

A heavy sergeant with a big moustache asked, "What kind of tree do you want?"

Sergeant Robbins told him we were shopping for the service club and handed him Mrs. Kline's note with the exact measurements and physical requirements.

"She gives me the same instructions every year. Come and have a look at these. This whole stack fits the bill. He led them to a row of firs that resembled huge majestic green animals lying helplessly on their sides.

The fresh foresty odor tickled Shannon's nostrils.

The sergeant held up several of the largest trees and they chose a fine full fir.

The two sergeants carried the tree to the truck and Sergeant Robbins and Shannon returned to the club.

Mrs. Kline was enchanted with the tree. "I knew you could do it," she said.

"I couldn't have chosen a better one myself. Isn't that a beauty, Sergeant Robbins?"

"She's lovely," Sergeant Robbins, said looking at Shannon.

Marcella had some beautiful creative ideas for decorating the tree, but Mrs. Kline insisted that the boys liked to do it themselves. Christmas was the one time she let the men have a say in decorating the club.

Marcella had another idea for the tree, "Why don't we let each airman make or choose one instrument he wants to put on the tree?"

"That is going too far," Mrs. Kline said. She laughed. "You don't know the boys. If we told them they could each bring their own decoration they would bring in women's stockings and underwear and anything vulgar you can imagine. They would insist that we put whatever they brought on the tree.

"As for creating their own, they are nice boys but they are not creative or artistic. They would make some awful ugly things and be hurt if we did not use them. No. We'll do things the way we always have. The three of us will get out

all the old decorations and see what new ones we need. Then one of us will go shopping for whatever is missing. When we have everything ready we will have a decorating party. We will serve coffee and doughnuts and eggnog and fruit cake and sing Christmas carols. It's a beautiful night when we are all decorating the tree. I always look forward to it."

The service club carpenter went into the storeroom and brought out all the old boxes of decorations. He was a short, energetic man with a slight limp. He looked at the large Father Christmas that hung on the wall. The service club artist had drawn and painted it. "What does that Communist know about Christmas?" he asked. "I don't understand how you Americans can keep a Communist on the base."

"He's not really a Communist," Marcella said.

"You don't know the half of it," the carpenter said, frowning. "I wouldn't be surprised if he were a spy. I keep warning Mrs. Kline but she won't listen. Nobody listens to me. Just wait until it's too late. Then they will all be sorry."

He stood his head and limped away to get another box.

The artist had heard him. He came hurrying out of his studio. His heavy body swollen under his white apron. "What's that Fascist saying about me?" he shouted. "He hates me because I know what he really is. He talks about me being on the base. I never fought against the Americans. Ask him what he was going when the Nazis took over France? Just ask him."

He returned to his studio.

"Those two!" Marcella said. "When will they ever sign a truce?"

The Christmas tree decorating party was a big success. There was a large crowd in the club, both white and black airmen and since there was no dancing there was no problem.

Mrs. Kline played all her favorite Christmas records. Everyone helped decorate the tree and they drank coffee and tea and ate homemade cookies.

Before the night ended they sang "Hark the Herald Angels Sing," "Frosty the Snowman" and "Silent Night." Shannon started to think of how wonderful it would be to be home for Christmas. The Christmas lights, the men's laughter and the snow drops falling helped her begin to enjoy the Christmas spirit.

Tis the Season to
Wrap up your dreams
And tie them to your heart
Or to the heart of another
Pilgrim following the star
Or a planet
Looking for a home.

Chapter Six
Tis the Season

Shannon's sister Jeanette and her fiancé Frank met her at the airport in Columbus. Ohio. The weather was bitter cold and Shannon was glad she had her heavy winter coat. The ground was covered with snow and a few snowflakes were still falling.

Jeanette and Shannon threw their arms around each other. "I've really missed you," they said at once.

"It's so good you've agreed to be my bride's maid. It wouldn't have felt right to get married without my one and only sister."

When they reached the house, Shannon felt a strong feeling of homecoming. She had grown up in this house. She remembered the ticking of the beautiful Grandfather's clock, the warn, but eloquent sofa and matching chair, and the warm fire in the fireplace. She was shocked to see how old her parents had become in less than two years. Her mother had prepared a big meal with her favorite foods,

baked potatoes, a green bean casserole and fried chicken with pumpkin pie for dessert.

Shannon slept in her old room and it brought back many powerful memories, some delightful and some sad. Where had that little girl gone who used to sleep in this bed and have her parents read her a story each night? It made her sad to think that she would never live here again and that the little girl she once was no longer existed.

It made her happy to think of her sister Jeanette and Frank. They both seemed so happy about the wedding. It was easy to see that they were deeply in love.

Shannon wondered if she would ever fall in love.

Jeanette took Shannon shopping for her bride's maid's dress. She had five bride's maids so she wanted to make sure there were five dresses available in the correct sizes. They choose a lovely red velvet gown. It fit Shannon beautifully and Jeanette felt confident there were identical dresses that would fit the other women.

The two sisters took a break from shopping and had lunch together in a diner where they used to hang out when they were teenagers.

"I can't believe it," Shannon said, "This place hasn't changed since we were kids. They even have the same old juke box. Let me see if they still have my favorite songs."

She put her money in the slot. "Can you believe it? My songs are still here!"

Elvis was still singing "It's Now or Never." "I haven't heard that song for years. That's the song Larry and I used to dance to."

Just then a nice looking young man came towards her. "Shannon," he said, "I saw you come in with Jeanette and I thought that was you but I haven't seen you for years."

"Larry? Is it really you?" she asked.

'It's me all right, "he said. "Where have you been keeping yourself? Last time we spoke, you were going away to college. I was away myself for awhile. I joined the navy and saw the world and now I'm back home."

She gave him a quick description of her life during the last six years.

She found herself excited by his presence. She had never felt that emotion before with him or with anyone else for that matter.

When Jeanette said hello to Larry, he said, "I hear you and Frank are getting married. That's great."

"I think so," she said.

The jukebox finished playing "It's Now or Never" and began "Love is a Many Splendored Thing."

"Remember how we always used to dance to this," Larry said. "Shall we?'

"Love to," Shannon said, putting her arms around him. He looked at Shannon with so much feeling it was as though there was no one else in the room.

Jeanette sat sipping a coke as she watched her sister Shannon dancing with her high school sweetheart.

Shannon felt she had stepped inside a time machine and been taken back to her high school years. She remembered how she had missed Larry when he went away to college and she surprised herself how happy she was to see him again.

When the song ended, Shannon invited Larry to have a drink with her and her sister. He was all too happy to spend more time with her.

Jeanette started asking Larry what he had been doing since they saw him last. He said, "I went to Ohio University where I played football and studied engineering. After I graduated I joined the Navy. I traveled a lot, saw some interesting places and last year I got out of the Navy and returned to Columbus. Since them I've been helping my father in his shop."

Larry was delighted when Jeanette invited him to the wedding.

When Shannon and Jeanette were leaving, Larry took Shannon's hand and held it as if he was never going to let go.

He held her hand all the way to Jeanette's car. "See you," he said.

"Yes, see you."

When they got home, Shannon went to her room. She sat down and looked around her. She couldn't understand what was happening to her. Why had seeing her childhood friend excited her? This certainly wasn't love at first sight. They had seen each other every day for years when they were growing up. But she had to admit she has never felt this way before.

The next morning Larry came by to take Shannon to breakfast. He was driving his BMW and wearing a blue cashmere sweater that brought out the blue of his large eyes.

Shannon was surprised to see him. She was wearing an old pare of blue jeans and a black turtleneck sweater. If she had any idea he was coming she would have carefully chosen an outfit that flattered her.

They went back to the diner where they had run into each other the day before.

"I thought you said you were working with your dad. What time do you have to go to work?"

"I usually start work at 9a.m. but I told my father I was taking you to breakfast and he told me to take as much time as I wanted."

"So how long are you staying in Ohio?' he asked.

"I work in the Air Force service club in Evruex, France, not far from Paris and I have to work on New Year's Eve."

"That's not very long," he said.

"I would have liked to spend more time but I didn't want to miss my sister's wedding. She's asked me to be her main bride's maid."

"Are you romantically involved with anyone there?" he asked.

"No, I'm still a free spirit."

"What about you?"

"I've been dating several women from time to time but there's nothing serious."

They each ordered a big breakfast with eggs and bacon, biscuits and coffee.

They were more interested in each other than in the food.

"I can't believe it's really you," he said. "You know, Shannon, I have loved you ever since you were a little girl standing in front of the oncoming train and I had to jump on top of you to get you off the track."

"I wish I had more time here. It's going to be hard to get on that plane in less than two weeks."

"Well, let's enjoy the time we have together," he said.

They made plans to see each other as often as possible.

When he pulled up in front of her parents' house, Shannon quickly kissed him on the cheek, said goodnight and got out of the car.

He smiled and waved, waited until she was inside the house, then drove away.

Shannon spent most of her time helping Jeanette prepare for her wedding.

It was to take place December 27th at St. Mary's Catholic Church and the reception was to be at the Country Club.

Jeanette and Shannon went shopping for shoes, jewelry, stockings and clothes for the honeymoon. Jeanette and Frank were going to Tahiti for their honeymoon and she needed a suitcase, nightgown, swim suit, outfits for the tropics.

Shannon and Larry did manage to see each other every day. They brought each other up to date with what had been happening in their lives. Shannon found Larry such an easy person to talk to.

One evening she went to his place and they cooked supper together. She brought a fragrant bouquet of multi-colored wild flowers. He admired them and put them in a crystal vase. He put on some old records playing the songs

they had enjoyed when they were younger. She sliced tomatoes, onions, radishes for a salad.

They had a glass of champagne from his refrigerator. He had cooked a pot roast and checked it from time to time.

They had always felt comfortable together. They felt free to discuss almost any subject or to sit quietly together and enjoy one another's presence.

However, when Larry asked her, "Is it true Frenchmen are good lovers?" She laughed and said, 'They're okay." That was the first time she had lied to Larry. She didn't want him to know that she was a virgin, after all she was 26 years old.

"I've dreamed of making love with you for years."

She looked at him straight in the eyes and smiled. She walked over to him and threw her arms around him. He took her hand and led her into his bedroom.

He was surprised to find it so difficult. But he was very patient and gentle with her. Her eyes were full of tears. "I don't want to hurt you," he said.

She would have put up with any pain when it was mixed with the joy she felt when he held her close and she melted into him.

"Tell me the truth, Shannon. Is this your first time?"

She shook her head yes. "I didn't want you to know."

"You can't know how happy this makes me," he said. "I have loved you so long. I know this must have been painful for you but I promise it will be better next time." She lay in his arms after he fell asleep. She forced herself to wake him so he could drive her home because she did not want her parents to worry about her.

When she stepped outside, she stood there for a moment admiring the full moon. The sky was full of stars and yet the night was dark and cold. The ground was still covered with snow.

Larry held her in his arms as they sat in the car. "I hate to let go of you," he said.

"It's late," she said.''My parents will be waiting for me." She kissed him deeply and then slipped out of his arms and ran up the stairs.

Her parents were sitting in the living room on the sofa in front of the fire place.

"How was your evening?" her mother asked.

"I had a wonderful time."

"You're spending a lot of time with Larry," her father said.

"Larry's always been my best friend," she said.

Shannon joined her parents and they spoke of Jeanette's plans for the wedding and how they would miss Shannon once she returned to Europe.

After a short time, she excused herself and went to her bathroom where she bathed. Her body seemed different to her. "I'm not a virgin anymore." She dried herself and put on her flowered flannel nightgown. She brushed her teeth and then brushed her hair.

Then she lay down on the old fashioned bed that had once been her grandparents and had been hers while she was growing up. She closed her eyes, expecting to fall asleep immediately the way she usually did, but sleep did not come.

She lay there thinking of Larry, pretending he was holding her. She could still see his face and the loving way he looked at her.

She dreamed they were teenagers again, back dancing at the prom to "It's Now or Never" sung by Elvis.

When Larry came to pick her up the next day, Shannon ran down the steps.

He was standing at the bottom of the stairs. Neither of them spoke. Their eyes were linked. She hurried to him until they stood face to face; he drew her close to him and they clung to one another.

"How do you feel today?" he asked.

"Wonderful," she said.

The days rushed by and soon it was time for the wedding and in a few more days Shannon would be

returning to Europe. She couldn't imagine leaving Larry behind.

Jeanette looked wonderful in her wedding gown. Shannon had never seen Frank looking so handsome. They really were a great couple. She hoped they would be happy together.

The little church was crowded. Larry was there, looking sexy in his grey suit, white shirt and light blue tie. She had never seen him really dressed up before and the sight was delightful. She wished it was Larry and her getting married.

The reception was held in the country club. There was a live band and the place was decorated with multicolored flowers and streamers. The first music was romantic and then lively. Many people were dancing. Shannon's first few dances were with the best man. Then Larry joined her and they danced most of the dances together.

Jeanette and Frank looked so happy together. They fed each other cake and deliberately got cake all over themselves. When they held each other to dance, Shannon knew that they felt the same way that she and Larry felt about each other.

If only she and Larry could have been getting married.

Jeanette deliberately threw her bouquet into Shannon's arms. Shannon held the flowers to her chest. She wasn't superstitious but she hoped the bouquet was a promise that she would be the next one to get married.

That evening Jeanette and Frank left for their honeymoon. Shannon and Larry took a long walk though the neighborhood, enjoying each other's company.

"I can't believe it's time to return to the base," she said.

"Don't go," Larry said, "Stay here with me. Let's get married."

"I would love to marry you, but I'm supposed to work on New Year's Eve." she said, "I gave my word I would be

back for that. A lot of homesick airmen are counting on me."

"I will be homesick without you," Larry said.

"Me too."

Let us say
Our say
In a few words
Leaving today
Returning when I can
Email me
Email has replaced
Telegrams
In most cases
But I haven't learned
how to email money
Or my heart.

Chapter Seven
Email my heart

The dreaded day finally arrived and Larry took Shannon to the airport. It was snowing and she shivered in her heavy coat. "When will you come back?" he asked. "You will marry me, won't you?"

"Yes, I will marry you. And I will return as soon as I can get away gracefully,"

"It will be hard waiting,"

"I know," she said. "It will be hard for me too."

He kissed her goodbye right before she went through security and he stood there watching her move farther and farther away from him.

As she approached her gate, Shannon felt more alone than she ever had before. She asked herself why she hadn't

told Larry she would marry him right now and called Mrs. Kline to tell her she wasn't coming back. But she had given her word to work on New Year's Eve. And she shouldn't give up her job without notice. She decided to give notice as soon as she arrived.

When she finally got her seat on the plane, Shannon began reading her nook, "An American Poetry Anthology." The book helped her relax and she was almost asleep when the Stewardess brought her meal.

She had a choice between filet of sole and fried chicken. She chose the chicken and enjoyed the meal. After dinner, she read her book for awhile and then fell asleep.

An anouncement from the pilot in the cockpit awakened her. She looked at her watch. It was two a.m. "Fasten your safety belts," the voice said. "We are having some very intense weather."

Shannon fastened her seat belt and went back to sleep. But in a short time the plane's rocking back and forth woke her up. The seat belt sign was still flashing.

The stewardess were trying to serve drinks but the plane was shaking so bad they had to return to their seats and the few people who had received drinks could not drink them because they were spilling on their clothes.

Shannon had never before flown during such a bad storm. She tried to read her book but her hands shook. In fact the entire plane shook.

Everyone on the plane was beginning to feel afraid. Some people were praying aloud. Others were crying. Children were asking, "Are we going to crash? Are we going to die?"

Their parents tried to calm them, promising they would be okay but no one was too sure. Then to make everything worse, the pilot announced that the plane could not land in Paris as originally scheduled because there was a strong blizzard there. They would be landing in Barcelona, Spain instead.

Shannon wondered how she would get from Barcelona to Evruex. She assumed the plane company would arrange that. If the plane would just stop shaking.

Finally she was able to relax and read some poetry. Just as she started to slip into sleep, there was another announcement, "We just learned that there is a storm in Barcelona so we can't land there."

Where would they land? Everyone was asking. Some people were shouting.

Shannon read her book and tried not to think of the situation. Surely the pilot and crew could figure out where to land. This could not be the first time they were flying into a storm.

"Stewardess," a woman shouted. "I have to have some water to take my pill."

"Can you wait a little while?" the stewardess asked. "The plane is shaking and we may spill the water."

"I have to take my pill," the woman shouted.

The stewardess came with a glass of water that was spilling on her and the floor.

The woman took her pill and got more water on her dress than in her mouth.

Everyone was nervous, restless, moving around, muttering, whispering. A baby started yelling at the top of its voice. Shannon felt sorry for the mother who was having no luck quieting the child. She tried not to listen to the shriek. It seemed to make everything look worse.

Shannon wondered if she was going to die. What will happen to me? She said an Act of Contrition. "Oh my God, I am hardly sorry for having offended thee. I detest all my sins because I dread the loss of Heaven and the pains of hell, but most of all because they offend thee, my God, who art all good and deserving of my love. I firmly resolve with the help of thy divine grace to confess my sins, do my penance and amend my life Amen."

Whenever Shannon went to confession she would end by saying the Act of Contrition and the nuns had told her when she was in school that if she was ever in danger of death she should say that prayer with all her heart and God would forgive her for any sin she had committed.

She thought how sad Larry would be if the plane crashed and he never saw her again. And how distressed her Mom and Dad and Jeanette would be. She would miss them so very much.

She wondered if she would see her grandparents when she got to Heaven.

When they died her mother had promised her she would join them in Heaven one day.

Would she go to Purgatory? She had once asked a Catholic priest who was born in India if he believed in Reincarnation and the priest said, "What do you think Purgatory is? Could it be possible that some people do come back to earth again and again. Could that be Purgatory? And if not what exactly was Purgatory?

No one alive really knows what death is. And people describe it many different ways. People who have had near death experiences while being operated on, or having a heart attack or stoke described a tunnel with light at the end of it.

Shannon wondered if she would see a tunnel.

The plane began rocking like a ship during a rough storm and Shannon prayed silently.

Another announcement said the plane would be landing in London since all the other airports in Europe were having blizzards.

Shannon wondered why the pilot and crew kept announcing all their changes of plan. It was making her nervous and she was certain it was upsetting many of the passengers.

The passengers were asked to keep their seat belts on and to remain in their seats. A few people insisted they had to use the restroom and they staggered down the aisle. Some of them fell against the seats and other passengers helped them to get back up.

Finally around 6 a.m. came the announcement that the pilot had decided to land in Paris as originally scheduled since all airports in Europe including London were having storms at the moment.

At 8 a.m. the plane reached Paris and the passengers were told that in order to insure their safety, due to the fact that there was zero visibility, the plane would circle the airport until all the gasoline was gone.

The plane circled the airport for two hours and Shannon kept wondering how the pilot was going to land with zero visibility.

Shannon had never prayed very much. She believed in God and tried to be a good person but praying didn't come natural to her. Right now it was the most natural thing to do. She even spoke to all her family who had already died, begging them to help her and the plane to survive this landing.

When the plane finally did land, she was astonished to see all the ambulances lined up around the airport in case there had been a problem.

Sergeant Robbins were there waiting for her. "Thank God, you are safe," he said. "I have never seen anything like it. I was here at 8 a.m when you were supposed to land and I watched your plane circling. You must have been terrified.

She laughed. "That wasn't the half of it. I have never had a flight like that and I hope I never have another."

There was a blizzard and the ground was covered with snow. The snow was still falling.

"I hope we make it safely to the base," she said.

"The worst is over," he promised her. "We will soon be home. Everyone on the base is waiting for you to help us celebrate New Year's Eve."

She wondered if God might be trying to tell her she should have stayed in Ohio with Larry. But she was back in Europe now and she would do her best to see that those lonely homesick airmen brought in the New Year with joy in their hearts.

Friends in pain
Can threaten you
Their cries of woe
Become roars of hatred
In spite of the love behind them
The more you love the friend
The deeper the wound
Friends about to fall
Can knock you off
Your Pedestal
Friends who are lost
Can lead you astray
But life without friends
Is empty space.

Chapter Eight
Friends

Ellie was happy to see that Shannon was back home. They had a glass of champagne to celebrate the holidays and Ellie told Shannon of her wonderful first Christmas as Frank's wife. She was delighted when Shannon told her all about her time with Larry and her plans to get married in a few months.

"I'll miss you," Ellie said, "but I am so happy for you."

"And I'll miss you, Ellie. I'm so glad we have shared this place."

When Shannon entered the service cub on December 31st, she was happy to see bright colored decorations and lights in every room. The Christmas tree was still standing and there were multi-colored packages underneath it.

Bing Crosby was singing "White Christmas" followed by Nat King Cole's "Christmas Song."

Everyone in the club seemed happy to see Shannon. "Welcome, home!" "Happy New Year!" "We were afraid you wouldn't come back!"

She wanted to tell them she would soon be leaving but she didn't want to spoil their New Year's Eve and she knew they loved to have American women working in the club.

Mrs. Kline must have feared Shannon would not return because she too was delighted to see her back. She came running out of her office and gave Shannon a big hug. "I'm so glad you're home," she said. "We are having some delicious food catered to the service club and I've hired a band with a singer."

Mrs. Kline had arranged for some excellent prizes, watches, boxes of candy, and billfolds to encourage the men to take part in all the games she had prepared for them. They had a pool tournament, chess game, table tennis and poker.

Shannon missed Larry. She wondered what he was doing on New Year's Eve. She wished she could have stayed in Ohio with him. She was eager to tell Mrs. Kline that she would be leaving to get married but she knew how disappointed she would be so she decided to wait until January 2nd after the holidays.

Well, 1965 would be here in less than twenty-four hours. She prayed it would be a year of peace and happiness. If all went as planned it would be her year to get married and live happily ever after.

She wondered what her sister Jeanette and her husband Frank were doing to celebrate the new year. She knew her Mom and Dad always went out to dinner and came

home and watched the New Year's Eve celebration at Times Square on their television.

The musicians arrived. Mrs. Kline had chosen a band with a beautiful French woman who sang in English. She was wearing a shiny silver dress that showed off her beautiful figure without being immodest. The men loved her. She had a lovely voice and sang popular American songs, mixing Christmas carols with other well-known songs.

Shannon looked around the room at all the airmen laughing and talking and having fun. She knew that many of them had been away from home for a long time and were homesick. She felt glad to be there helping them enjoy the beginning of a new year, 1965.

She dreamed she was back home in Larry's arms. One day in the near future she would be back in Ohio and her dream would come true.

Next morning Shannon had to get up and prepare for work. It was a holiday and she had to make certain that the men who had remained on the base would be comfortable.

When she stepped outside, Shannon was happy to see the sun was shining brightly although snow was falling heavily. The sun didn't do much to warm up the air but it helped raise her spirits. She loved to see the sun.

Once inside the service club she put on the coffee pot, opened the refrigerator and got out the orange juice. The delivery man brought the doughnuts and she prepared the table, putting out glasses, cups and napkins.

Mrs. Kline wished Shannon, "Happy New Year," poured herself a cup of coffee and brought it into her office with her.

Sergeant Robbins stopped by and drank a cup of coffee. "It's good to have you back in the service club," he said.

"It's good to be back," she said.

Several airmen came for their coffee and doughnuts.

Shannon was surprised to look up and see Regina entering the club.

"Hello," Shannon said, "I thought you were in Spain."

"I was in Spain," Regina said. "Ben and I are making arrangements to get married but I missed little Kathy so much. I had to check on her, to see if she's okay and I'm going to beg to take her back with me."

"Good luck," Shannon said.

"I thought I would be okay without her," Regina said. "But I can't stop worrying about her."

"Have a cup of coffee," Shannon said.

She poured a cup for Regina. "I stopped by the house this morning. Kathy was still asleep and Tom was just waking up, still drunk from last night. He told me to get the hell out of there and I figured I better listen to him because he can be really mean when he's drunk."

Shannon collected the prizes that had not been used and set up the games for the airmen who were in the club. Mrs. Kline joined her. She put on some Christmas music and announced that the games were beginning.

Sergeant Tom, Regina's husband staggered into the club. "Where is that bitch?" he shouted. "Regina! So that officer can't satisfy you and you came back to me?"

She was sitting alone at a table drinking her coffee and looking at a magazine. She started walking towards him. He pulled out a gun and shot her three times. She fell to the floor. Mrs. Kline and Shannon ran towards her.

Sergeant Tom started out the door.

Regina was still alive but she was bleeding heavily. The ambulance took her to the hospital. Some airmen held Tom until the M.P's came to arrest him.

"What a way to begin the New Year," Shannon said to Mrs. Kline.

"We have never had anything like this in the Service Club," she said. "I am so upset."

"Let's put on some more Christmas carols and get the men playing some games."

The next day Shannon told Mrs. Kline she was going to quit her job and return to Ohio to get married.

"Oh, no!" Mrs. Kline said, "I need you here. The men need you. I think of you like a daughter and I was hoping you could take over the club once I am too old to run it."

"That's kind of you," she said. "And I have really enjoyed working with you. But when I was in Ohio I connected with my childhood sweetheart and we've decided to get married. It's definite I'm giving you my notice now."

"How long can you stay?"

"How about two weeks?"

"Let's make it three, okay?"

"Okay."

That afternoon when she left the club, Shannon went to the hospital to see Regina. She was told her room number but when she got there, the room was empty. She asked a nurse what happened.

"They are operating on her," the nurse said. "It looks like they may have to remove one leg."

"Oh, no," Shannon said. "May I wait in the room for her?"

"You are welcome to wait, but it could be a long time."

"Thank you I'll wait." She knew it would help Regina to have company after the surgery.

It was several hours before they brought Regina back to her room. She was barely conscious due to all the medication. Shannon took her hand and said, "Regina, I'm here for you." Shannon couldn't tell whether or not one leg was missing.

Regina mumbled something and went to sleep. Shannon thought sleep was the best thing for her right then.

"I'm be back tomorrow," She said as she left.

When she got home, Ellie was there, "I was working when that poor woman came in," she said. "Her husband shot her. They tried to save her leg but it was hurt too badly."

"Yes, I was in the Service Club when he shot her. He was drunk and couldn't even walk straight. Thank God he didn't kill her."

The next day everyone on the base was talking about the shooting, Tom's being arrested and Regina in the hospital. Shannon learned that Tom's next door neighbors who had two children of their own were taking care of Regina's daughter Kathy.

Marcella was back at work after her holiday vacation and after work, she and Shannon went to the hospital together to visit Regina.

Regina was awake this time, She was very glad to see the two women and she told them, "I lost a leg. I don't know how I will manage but I would gladly give up my leg to have my daughter with me. And now that Tom has been arrested he can't keep me from my little girl. So it is worth it."

Marcella was also disappointed to learn that Shannon was leaving the club but she rejoiced with her about her marriage. Mrs. Kline could not stop begging Shannon to change her mind and remain with her at the club.

The days were full but they went too slowly for Shannon. Larry called her once a week and each time she put down the phone they seemed farther apart and she was more eager to be in his arms.

On January 23rd Sergeant Robbins drove Shannon to the Evreux airport.

"Have a good trip," he said. They both remembered how rough her last trip to Evreux had been. He gave her a big hug, kissed her on the cheek and said, "It's been a privilege knowing you. Thanks so much for making the Service Club a home for everyone."

"I just did my job the way I saw it. Goodbye, Sergeant Robbins. Thanks for all your help. It's been good knowing you."

When he walked away and she entered the plane she had a heavy moment thinking how her life as she'd known it was now ending. A new life was beginning.

While she looked forward to being Larry's wife the idea was a little frightening.

Home
Where we start from
Where we always
Yearn to return
Home
A place in the heart
Where the heart can rest.

Chapter Nine
Home

Shannon and Larry were married in St. Mary's Catholic Church where Jeanette and Frank had been married earlier. They had chosen to have a simple ceremony with only Jeanette as the Maid of Honor and Larry's best friend as best man. The priest read the service and Shannon and Larry's friends listened, many surprised by the marriage since Shannon had been gone for so long. Jeanette had a beautiful strong voice and she sang "Ave Maria."

After the ceremony, the friends and neighbors threw rice and gathered to shake hands with the groom or kiss the bride. Then everyone joined the wedding party in the parish hall for cake and wine or juice.

Shannon's parents were glad to have her back in the United States and hoped that she and Larry would remain close to them as Jeanette and Frank had chosen to do. But Larry was offered a high paying job in California, as superintendent of a big Construction company. He felt it would be interesting and fulfilling as well as financially satisfying so he asked Shannon if she would agree for him to take it.

Shannon had been to San Diego once and loved the city so she found it easy to agree to go there.

They rented a cute little white house in San Diego. Shannon made friends with her next door neighbor Annie, who went shopping with her for curtains, rugs, etc to decorate her home.

Larry enjoyed his work. He was a friendly, easy going person and he was very popular.

Shannon got a job teaching French at UCSD, University of California at San Diego.

She was glad to keep up with her French and the school directors were happy to have someone who had studied at the Sorbonne and spoke French with a Parisian accent.

When they had been in California for only six months, Shannon received a call while she was teaching. Larry had been in an accident at work. A wall had fallen and he and two of his men were knocked down under it. Shannon rushed to the hospital where he had been taken.

Larry was in a semi-coma. She tried to talk to him but he couldn't speak.

Larry's parents were dead. All he had was a sister Loretta. Shannon called her and she promised to come out immediately. She called her family and learned for the first time that her mother was suffering from Alzheimer's disease and her father was taking care of her. Jeanette got on a plane that day and arrived in San Diego that evening.

"I'm so glad you could come," Shannon told Jeanette, "This is so terrible and on top of it to learn that Mom has Alzheimer's."

"Yes," Jeanette said, "Mom's been suffering from it for quite some time. We were hoping you wouldn't notice it. We didn't want to spoil your wedding."

"I understand but I wish I had known. I just ignored Mom when I was home paying attention only to Larry."

"That's young love," Jeanette said. "It's natural to focus on the one you love especially during your wedding."

Shannon and Jeanette spent most of their time in the hospital with Larry waiting for him to come out of the coma. After a week, Larry regained consciousness but he had great difficulty speaking. When he recognized Jeanette, he asked her to sing "Ave Maria," the song she sang at the wedding.

Jeanette looked at Shannon questioning. Shannon said, "Yes, please sing it." Larry smiled and looked so content as Jeanette put her heart into the song. Shannon had a difficult time controlling her emotions. She had felt so wonderful when her sister sang that song at her wedding, now it pulled at her heart strings. She was so afraid she was losing her beloved husband. Seeing how happy "Ave Maria" had made Larry, Jeanette asked if she could sing something else. He shook his head yes and with great difficulty said "Love is A many Splendored Thing." This song took Shannon back to her high school romance with Larry.

Larry's sister Loretta arrived just in time to say goodbye to him. Shannon, Jeanette, and Loretta gathered around Larry. He recognized his sister but wasn't able to say anything to her. He did manage to say "Ave Maria" to Jeanette and she sang for him. Loretta cried aloud as Jeanette sang. Shannon cried inside. Larry fell asleep and the nurse suggested they all go home and get some rest and come back early in the morning. Shortly after they left the room Larry died.

Larry had signed papers that he had been in the Navy and wanted to be buried at sea. So the Neptune society helped with the arrangements for his memorial service. He was cremated and Shannon was given a beautiful Urn with his ashes. The little crowd of mourners gathered inside a boat. There was the Catholic priest from Shannon and Larry's new parish, Jeanette, Loretta, Shannon, her friend Annie, her co-worker Lynda, a young sailor and the men who were driving the boat.

Shannon handed each one a bouquet of fragrant bright colored flowers.

The priest said a few words then Shannon spoke and then Loretta.

Jeanette sang "Ave Maria" and Shannon removed the American flag from the Urn and threw the Urn into the ocean.

She tossed a lei of plumeria flowers after the Urn and invited everyone to throw their bouquet into the water.

The young sailor played Taps.

As the little boat headed back to shore minus its most important treasure Shannon watched the Urn toss in the water next to the lei surrounded by the garden of flowers left by he mourners.

Jeanette was missing her husband and wanted to return home as soon as possible. She begged Shannon to come with her but Shannon didn't want to leave her school. She had started to feel at home in California. But she promised to come home for Christmas to see how her mother was doing and to spend time with Jeanette and Frank.

Shannon went back to work teaching French at the University. She felt good to keep herself busy. But each day when she got home in an empty house she felt lonely and lost. How could she go on without her beloved Larry? If only they could have had children.

One day she was speaking with Lynda, the woman who taught Spanish next door to the French class. Lynda said, "I'm taking a writing class after school. Harold Dunlap teaches it. He's a great writer, has published many books, won a Pulitzer prize and he's a wonderful teacher. He gives me confidence, makes me feel I can write even if I never did before. Why don't you come check the class out with me? It would give you something interesting to do, help you avoid being so sad."

Shannon went to the class with Lynda the next evening. Herald was a tall, thin handsome man with curly blond hair and deep blue eyes. He wore black slacks and a light blue cashmere sweater.

Harold was very informal. He said, "Anyone who can write a letter can write a book. All you have to do is sit at your typewriter or computer and keep hitting the keys. Eventually you will create something others can read and you can feel good about it."

Shannon wrote a few lines in class. "You will never get the truth if you think you know ahead of time what the truth should be. There are many people inside each of us and we must allow all their voices to express themselves if we want to begin to know our personal truth."

When she read them, Harold said, "That's wonderful. You have a real talent. So glad you decided to develop it."

When she got home Shannon prepared for her French class and wrote an essay for her writing class. It felt good to be busy. She was so glad she had decided to take the class.

Harold had said, "Writing can help you understand the inner meaning of your life, what is important, why and how." That statement had fascinated her. She had never thought about the inner meaning of her life, but now, thanks to Harold she was wondering.

Another time he said, "Writing can be a form of therapy, a form of meditation, a way of spiritual and psychological healing and growth."

Inspired by his descriptions, Shannon hurried to her computer each evening after class and soon had a good start on a book.

Harold said, "A biographer needs to be both humble and cautious when he remembers the nature of his material, for a historical fact is rather like the flamingo that Alice in Wonderland tried to use as a mallet for croquet. It kept looking at her with a puzzled expression and what we call a fact has a way of looking at us that way."

Every evening Shannon would call her parents to see how her mother was doing. Shannon had heard terrible things about Alzheimer's so she was relieved to be able to

speak with her mother and find that she sounded the same as she always had.

Shannon enjoyed teaching French to her students who seemed to find the class interesting.

Shannon worked on her book each night when she got home. She called it A Hard Rain, inspired by Bob Dylan's song "A Hard Rain is Gonna Fall." The writing filled her evenings and gave her a feeling of accomplishment. She didn't know if she would ever try to publish it, or even share it with the writing class but she was so glad she had begun writing.

She always found Harold's classes inspiring. He began each class with a few words of inspiration. "Today's word of wisdom comes from Samuel Beckett: 'Try Again. Fail again. Fail better.' In other words the more you fail, the closer you come to succeeding."

He would invite any student to read a sample of his or her writing, not going over 20 minutes. Before each class Shannon carefully prepared a few pages of her best writing but once in class she decided it wasn't good enough or she was too nervous to read or she would rather read something else next time.

Harold was very good at allowing each student to choose his or her own rhythm and did not force anyone to read against their will.

In each class Harold gave a short lecture on the art of writing. "Is it true that writers always begin with clichés, describing the obvious, the expected? That is why we need to go deeper, to examine the details, to see life with our own eyes. Then we can give to our work what no one else can give, our vision, our unique way of seeing, hearing, feeling. That is why we must pay attention. Be present in our lives."

After class Shannon and her friend Lynda often stopped at a nearby restaurant for a soda and some girl talk.

"I think Harold is so cute," Lynda said.

"I hadn't noticed," Shannon said, "But he is a darn good teacher. He makes me want to rush home and begin writing."

At the next class Shannon found herself carefully examining Harold for the first time. She had been so interested in his words that she had not paid much attention to his appearance or his mannerisms. She agreed with Lynda he was very cute, handsome and charismatic. His voice was mellow and she really liked his smile which seemed to be in his eyes even more than on his mouth.

A few weeks later, Shannon and Lynda were having a cup of coffee and discussing the class and Harold's charms when Harold entered the restaurant.

Lynda jumped up and ran over to invite him to join Shannon and her.

He said, "Thanks so much, I'd love to join you. I'm only here for a quick coffee but I'd enjoy your company until I have to leave."

"It's always nice to see some of my students outside of class," he said, sitting down at their table. For the first time Shannon noticed how long his legs were.

"I'm really enjoying your class," Shannon said. "I have always wanted to write but I never have."

"Have you started writing now?" he asked.

"Oh, yes, I write every night. But I don't think I'm ready to share anything in class."

"Then I'm not doing my job," he said. "My goal is to make the class a safe refuge where everyone feels free to share anything they write."

'Oh, I do feel safe in your class. I find it so inspiring. I never would have been able to write anything if I hadn't been in your class. It's just than I'm a little shy. Not really shy, inhibited."

"I hope you will get over that," he said.

Then he turned to Lynda, "I've enjoyed the writing you've shared in class. Are you enjoying the class?"

"I love it," she said. "It makes my day."

The next day Shannon took a few pages of her manuscript to class. "This is the beginning of my book. It is called A HARD RAIN inspired by Bobby Dylan's song about "A Hard Rain is Gonna Fall." It is the story of some young Puerto Ricans who want their country to be free from America. It begins with some soldiers coming back from Vietnam.

Chapter One The Long Road Home

Most of the 5000 soldiers wounded in action came home via Germany, arms missing, legs missing, eyes missing, bodies given for their country for whose Freedom they gave themselves to the Glory of War, the Great Adventure.

The pain, the shock, the loss, missing so much of the body. Many are still alive because of the progress of American medicine. Wish we'd make progress in Peace.

Do they really want to live that way? Where is their freedom? They are learning how to live again. The truck went up in a ball of fire. A soldier drove the truck out of harm's way, saved a truckload of soldiers coming behind him. Going home."

""That's some powerful material, " Harold said. "Thank you so much for sharing it with us."

After class, Lynda and Shannon went to the restaurant as usual. "Let's get a hot fudge sundae to celebrate your reading your manuscript in class," Lynda said.

Shannon loved the idea. They were enjoying their ice-cream when Harold joined them. "Shannon, thank you so much for reading some of your work today. I really enjoyed it. For a first time writer you are very good."

She smiled and thanked him. "You are just too kind," she said.

"I'm honest," he said, "not kind."

He ordered his usual coffee and the three of them discussed the class.

Meeting in the restaurant after writing class became a habit for the three of them but it was several weeks before Harold began asking personal questions and the two women were happy to learn a little about him.

Harold asked Shannon about her life. She told him she was born in Ohio and had gone to the Sorbonne then got married and moved to California where she got a job teaching French and her husband was killed in an accident.

"I'm sorry to hear about your husband's accident," he said. "I know how you feel the love of my life died last year and the sorrow never ends" He smiled.

"It does lessen though."

Lynda started feeling like she didn't belong. She stayed that evening but after the next class she told Shannon she had some shopping to do and before Shannon started out the door Harold took her arm and the two of them were in the restaurant alone for the first time.

In my dearest dreams
I search for my heart
Forgetting that I handed it to you long ago
I'm am glad you nurtured my soul
And warmed my cold cold hands
You came into my life as a stranger
And now you are my all.

Chapter Ten
Searching for my heart…

"I've been looking forward to this day," Harold told her. "Lynda is an interesting woman but I have been longing to see you alone."

"It is nice to be alone," Shannon said.

"I've been wanting to ask you out," Harold said. "What about having dinner one night and then going to a movie?"

"That sounds like a good idea," Shannon said. "I haven't been out to eat or to a movie since my husband died."

"I know how you feel. Losing a loved one makes everything seem meaningless. Since I met you I have been finding meaning once more," he said.

"I am overwhelmed," she said. "I never thought there was a chance you could be interested in me so I never allowed myself to be interested in you. Now I feel overwhelmed."

"You will have dinner with me and we can choose a movie."

"Yes, I'm looking forward to it."

Their evening together was enchanting. They went to a small Italian restaurant with red and white checkered tablecloth, candles on every table and Italian opera music in the background. They had veal parmesan with a fresh green salad and red wine.

Afterwards they went to see a French movie, Au Bout de Souffle. When he brought her home, she invited him inside for coffee. He said, "Thank you so very much for spending this evening with me. It is the best time I've had since my lover died. But I feel I have not been fair to you. I can't ever make love to you even though I am longing to. You see, I have AIDS. I'm sorry I didn't tell you before but I want to finish the semester so I can't let anyone know. My doctor assured me my students won't catch AIDS from me unless we get close. So please forgive me."

"Oh, Harold, I am so sorry to hear you are sick."

"I guess this will be our last time together outside of school but I would appreciate it if you would not tell anyone about my illness."

"Harold, I care about you. I want to be your friend. We can continue going out together."

"That would be wonderful," he said. "I have been so lonely and I was afraid to get close to anyone."

Harold and Shannon went out together several times a week. They were falling in love but they wouldn't even kiss for fear she would catch the deadly disease that was killing him.

He appeared healthy until the day when he caught a cold and because his immune system was weak he got pneumonia and was in the hospital for two weeks. When he came out he was weak, had lost a lot of weight and no longer looked healthy.

Finally Harold gave up his teaching job and went home to write one last book before he died.

Shannon was still teaching her French class but she began to spend all of her free time at Harold's home, helping in any way she could. He had hired a cook and housekeeper so what he needed most was tender loving care.

Shannon loved to watch "Murder She Wrote" on television. She identified with J.B. Fletcher, a female writer, a widow living alone, visiting friends, traveling, with many friends. She would watch while Harold wrote. Shannon pretended she was as famous as Jessica with everyone knowing her writing and having all the money she needed to travel or buy a new electric typewriter.

Shannon brought her laptop to Harold's and they both worked on their books when he was strong enough.

The pain was almost physical when they longed to kiss one another with deep intimate kisses and to make love but they had to hold themselves back to make certain Shannon didn't catch his disease.

One day he told her, "Shannon, you are the first woman I ever loved and you are truly the love of my life. You know I am gay, don't you? Or I was gay all my life. Ronnie was the most important man in my life and he died of AIDS last year."

Shannon felt stunned. She had wondered if he was gay when he spoke of his lover, the love of his life. But she had not wanted to believe it so she had held on to the idea that he was an ordinary heterosexual man. But knowing that he had been gay all his life did not bother her anymore than learning that he had AIDS. She loved him and that was all there was to it. Nobody's perfect she told herself with a smile.

To complicate her life even more her sister Jeanette called to say their mother was rapidly losing her mind as the Alzheimer's destroyed it. She begged Shannon to come home while her Mother would still recognize her.

Harold was getting weaker all the time and the two of them were becoming closer all the time in spirit and in love. She told him about her mother and he encouraged her to go home and spend time with her mother.

"I'll be here when you return," he promised.

Lynda drove her to the airport and promised to look in after Harold while she was gone.

The plane ride was smooth and Jeanette and Frank picked her up at the airport and drove her to her parents' home.

When she entered the house, she saw her mother sitting on the sofa watching television. She walked up to her mother and her mother smiled and said, "Abigail, what are you doing here?" She thought Shannon was her own sister who had died several years ago.

"I'm Shannon," she told her mother. "I came home to see you."

"Shannon," she said. "What a lovely name. I had a daughter once named Shannon."

"I am your daughter," Shannon said, beginning to panic about her mother's memory.

She was glad she had come home before it was too late to communicate at all with her mother. It broke her heart to see her intelligent well-educated mother in such a sad state.

When Jeanette and Frank were visiting the house, Shannon put on some Broadway music and Jeanette began to sing along. Their mother joined them and sang every song. Shannon was amazed at how her mother could remember all the words.

One night when Shannon was home with her parents, her father bought the parts of a new computer that he decided to build on his own. He took all the parts and the directions into the master bedroom and asked Shannon to keep an eye on her mother while he was working on the computer placing all the pieces as directed.

Her dad ordered a large pizza and Shannon made a big spinach salad. Eager to get to work on the computer, her

dad ate a few pieces of pizza and a little salad and excused himself to start working on the computer.

Shannon and her mother took their time eating and had vanilla ice cream and coffee for desert. After dinner, they watched a rerun of the Waltons on television.

Around eight p.m., all the electricity went out. Shannon remembered that her mother had told her she keeps a big flashlight next to her bed. So she opened the bedroom door to go get the flashlight.

Her father shouted, "Keep the door shut! All the parts of the computer are scattered everywhere. Stay out and don't let your mother come in!"

"Dad, can you get a flashlight for us? It's on Mother's side of the bed, on her bed stand."

"I can't move," he said. "I put each piece in the order it needs to be used. I can't move or I will lose track of the pieces."

In the meantime from the kitchen came strange sounds as her mother knocked things off the shelves trying to find a way to get some light.

Shannon ran into the kitchen hoping to help her mother and prevent any more items from falling. As she entered the room, her mother knocked the phone off the stand.

"Why did Dad turn off the lights?" Her mother asked. "Doesn't he know we need some light? I don't understand that man. He's getting strange in his old age."

"Dad didn't turn off the lights, mom. The lights just went out. The electric company has to turn them on."

Her mother went on switching all the lights off and on and complaining that none of them were working.

Shannon led her mother into the living room and opened the curtains so they could get a little light from the street lights that were still burning. Shannon wondered if it was a blown fuse but then she noticed that their neighbors on both sides had no electricity. Not even their porch lights were on.

After a long search in the dark, Shannon found two candles but she was unable to find matches.

Her mother kept going from room to room trying all the switches and knocking things down.

Her dad kept the doors locked to the master bedroom.

He finally located the big flashlight her mother had told her about. He brought it into the living room so Shannon and her mother could find the things they were looking for. Then he held the light while Shannon looked up the phone number for the electric company and called them to say the lights were out.

They told her, "Yes, thank you for calling. We are aware of the problem. We are working on it right now. Your lights should be on in a few hours."

While her father was in the bedroom, carefully collecting all the parts of the soon-to-be-computer, in the dark living room, Shannon helped her mother into her nightgown.

Her father came out of the bedroom. "Well, I cleaned up the computer mess so the old lady and I can go to sleep now."

Shannon helped her mother into bed, tucked her in, and said a little prayer, "Now I lay me down to sleep I pray the Lord my soul to keep. If I should die before I wake I pray the Lord my soul to take."

She kissed her goodnight and slipped out of the room.

Shannon climbed the stairs to her bedroom in the dark, holding tight to the rail. She would have loved to have a candle or the flashlight her father was still using.

The upstairs floor seemed huge in the dark and Shannon walked with her hands on the wall searching for the door to her bedroom.

In the dark her room seemed strange. She fumbled around until she located the door to her closet and then felt all the clothes until she found her flannel gown. She slipped off her clothes and put on the night gown.

Shannon usually listened to music on her radio as she fell asleep. Without electricity she lay in the dark tossing and turning.

Just when she was finally falling asleep, the electricity came back on and all the lights in the house were shinning. The television was blasting because her mother turned it louder trying to get it to play with the electricity gone.

Shannon got out of bed and turned off the television and most of the lights; then she went into the dining room and cleared off the table.

When she was alone with her father he tried to bring her up to date on her mom's condition. "We have to watch her at all times. She tries to run away and once she is outside the house alone she gets lost. We had to call the police several times to help us find her. It's very dangerous if she gets in the street. She does not know how to relate to cars and she almost got run over several times. It's really hard to take care of her."

The most difficult for Shannon was the fact that most of the time her mother didn't know her. She'd call her Abigail as she did when Shannon first arrived or she would say, "I know I know you but I forget who you are." It made Shannon want to cry.

"Shannon, you must help me," her mother told her, "The doctor says I have Alzheimer's. I don't want to have Alzheimer's. Don't let me have it. Help me find something to keep me from getting Alzheimer's. I go to the Center and I see the people who have the disease and I don't want to be like them. They are strange.

"I don't want to be strange. I don't want to find myself wandering the hills, not even recognizing my own hands or feet or fingers with no memory, a vague sense of being expected somewhere, not knowing where. Meeting people out of your dreams. Promise me you won't let me have Alzheimer's."

"Mother, I can't promise to keep you from Alzheimer's but I promise to see that you are always taken care of. And

you will stay close to God and He will heal you in His own way. You can make it easier for God to heal you by taking good care of yourself. You must eat your meals and take your walks and get enough rest."

"Thank you for letting me know," her mother said.

And she worried about Harold. She called him every night. Some nights he sounded so weak and she longed to be there taking care of him.

One day when Shannon was preparing the tub for her mother, she put in some bubble bath and went to get towels and a wash clothe. When she returned to the bathroom, she found her mother sitting in the water with all her clothes on.

One morning her mother said, "I'm going to take my shower."

"Can I help you?" Shannon asked.

"No, thank you. When I take my shower I don't need help."

Shannon started cooking breakfast while her mother showered. She noticed that her mother had been in the shower for a long time so she went to check on her. Shannon discovered that her mother had forgotten to close the shower door and the floor was covered with water.

She helped her mother dry herself than led her into her bedroom and returned to dry the floor.

Her mother wanted to dress herself but she had a few problems.

So Shannon helped her get ready. Then Shannon finished cooking breakfast and served her parents.

Shannon went with her mother to the Alzheimer's center for a Hawaiian Luau. She and her mother wore their Mu Mus, Hawaiian bright colored long dresses withy various tropical flowers. The Center had hired a Hawaiian singer and two dancers. Their first song was "Where I live there are rainbows."

There was a crowd enjoying the show. One of the servers came into the room and said, "I forgot when I came for. Does that ever happen to any of you?"

Together, everyone shouted, "All the time."

In the middle of the night, Shannon's mother woke her up. "Get up. Get ready. It's time for church." She was wearing her bra over her nightgown and had her Easter bonnet on her head.

"Look out the window, Mom. It's night. It's too early for church and it isn't Sunday."

Her mother insisted that it was morning. She picked up the alarm clock and showed it to Shannon. "See it's time for church and it is Sunday. The clock says so."

When her father woke up he was worried to see that his wife got up alone while he was sleeping. "Thank God you were here, Shannon. If she was up by herself she might have run away again. That's why I may have to put her in a nursing home. I hate to think of it but I don't want anything to happen to her."

Shannon was torn between spending more time with her mother and returning to be with Harold. She was afraid he was going to die while she was away. She discussed the situation with Jeanette. "It sounds to me like you had better get back to California if you want to see your friend before he dies. Mother could live a long time. Her mind is no longer the way it was when we were growing up. It's good you got to see her."

Even though she didn't have to be back to school for two weeks, Shannon decided to return to California so she could see Harold.

Her friend Lynda met her at the airport. They hugged one another. "How is Harold doing?" Shannon asked.

"He isn't doing well at all," Lynda said. "I'm so glad you've come back. I was afraid he would die before you arrived."

"Is he that bad?"

"He is."

Lynda drove her to Harold's and left her there.

He had given her a key earlier. She entered the door and everything was quiet. She climbed up to his bedroom.

When she entered the room, she saw him lying in bed, asleep. He was so small and white she gasped. She longed to be in his arms but she did not want to wake him. She was exhausted after her long trip so she took a blanket, lay on the sofa in his bedroom and fell asleep right away.

Harold woke her up at 4 in the morning coughing as though he was going to choke to death. She jumped up and ran to him. He recognized her but he could not stop coughing. He was reaching for her and gasping. She patted him on the back and finally he stopped coughing and lay still gasping for breath. When he could talk at last, he threw his arms around her and said, "My darling, I missed you so much. I am so glad you are back."

"I know, darling," she said. "I missed you too. It's so good to see you again."

"How is your mother?"

"She doesn't even know me. It was so hard to see my brilliant mother losing her mind so rapidly."

"Thank God I still have my mind but I am losing my body so fast I do not recognize it from day to day."

"I have decided I want to call my parents and let them know I am dying. I want to say goodbye."

She couldn't believe she was hearing this. He had told her both of his parents were dead.

"I know I told you they were dead. When I told them I was gay they disowned me and said as far as they were concerned I was dead and they didn't want to see me again."

"I think it would be a wonderful idea for you to phone your parents. Maybe they will be more understanding now."

"They live in Massachusetts," he said as he dialed their number on his cell phone

"Hello, Dad. This is Harold. No, I'm not in Massachusetts. I'm still in San Diego. No, I'm not with him anymore. He died. Is Mother there? Can I speak to her?

"Hello, Mother. I just wanted to say hello. Or maybe I should say I wanted to say goodbye. I have AIDS and I'm

dying pretty soon now. I just wanted to hear your voice. I love you, Mom. I'm sorry that I upset you and Dad with my lifestyle.

"I know you love me. I miss you too. No, I'm too sick to come home. I don't think I am going to get any better but if I do I will try to come home. I understand San Diego is too far for you and Dad. You don't like planes and it's too far for a train.

I'm glad I could call. Maybe I'll call again. I love you Goodbye. Say goodbye to Dad." He had tears in his eyes.

"I'm glad I called them," he said. "But I don't think they will ever be able to forgive me for being gay."

"I guess they'd be happy to know you are in love with a woman," she said.

"I didn't want to mention that. My parents always wanted me to fall in love with a woman and get married and have grandchildren for them. Now that it's too late to have children I don't want them to know I'm in love with a wonderful woman who could have given them fabulous grandchildren."

"I think it's great that you called them. You can call them again in a day or two when you are feeling better."

"I don't know if I will ever feel better."

Looking at him, so pale, so weak, she didn't know either if he would ever get better.

When the nurse stopped by to check on Harold, Shannon used his car to drive home and get the mail that had collected and listened to the messages on her answering machine. She didn't want to be apart from Harold any longer than she needed to. She packed a suitcase with a night gown, changes of underwear, tooth brush and a few changes of clothes. Then she drove back to Harold's.

Shannon climbed in to bed besides Harold. "Let me know if it bothers you having me here and I'll sleep on the sofa like I did yesterday."

"I love having you here with me. I wish I could hold you close but my arms are so weak. But having you with me feels so good. I love you, you know."

"Yes, I know and I love you."

Shannon sat in Harold's living room. He was upstairs asleep. She looked at his many bookshelves and admired the books. Then she came across the books he had published, Write Your Heart out, a How to Write book, and three novels, Oh, Give Me a Home, The Brown Grass of Home and The Home fires.

She took the first novel, got comfortable on the sofa and began reading. He was a great teacher and she had assumed he would be a great writer. His writing was powerful. The characters came alive on the page. The plot was intriguing, fast moving and she couldn't wait to turn the page and read what happened next. The setting was so well described she felt she was there. She saw the bright colored flowers, heard the wind whistling in the trees, entered the houses, smelled the bread baking in the oven, felt the wool scratching a character's flesh and found herself inside the main character's soul.

Harold woke up and called her name. She was torn between wanting to continue reading his book and rushing to his side. That was a stupid thought she told herself. He needs me and there's nothing I want more than to be with him.

Harold was waiting for her in his bed. He was so weak he could hardly hold his head up. He reached out for her and she ran into his arms, lying next to him on his bed.

She kissed his cheek and asked, "How do you feel, my love?"

"I don't feel," he said. "It's almost as if I am already gone. Physically I feel nothing but my heart feels a lot. It is on fire with love for you."

"I am so happy your heart feels love for me because my heart is on fire for you but I do wish your body would join

us. You haven't eaten all day. Would you like a little chicken soup?

"I'm not hungry but to please you I will make an effort."

She rushed downstairs and into the kitchen where she choose a can of soup, heated it up on his stove and brought him a bowl of it."

She fed it to him as though he were her little baby. She pretended the spoon was a plane bringing him something delicious and she promised when he finished eating she would lie and hold him. He made an effort to eat because he wanted to please her but he had no appetite and his stomach was uncomfortable.

"I'm sorry," he said after a few bites. "I really can't eat anymore."

She smiled at him. "You did a good job. I'm so happy to see you eating something." She lay down next to him and they held each other with passion mixed with compassion. Even if he got healthier, they could never make love because his disease was fatal and they could not take a chance that she would get it.

At times, she felt that she would like to die when he did. She had lost one man she loved and she did not want to feel that pain again. But it would be suicide to share her body with Harold the way she wanted to. She knew that would be wrong. Besides, Harold was determined to see that she took no unnecessary chances.

While Shannon was out of town with her parents, Harold's doctor had convinced him to bring Hospice workers to help him in his last days. The Hospice nurse called or stopped by each day to make sure he had everything he needed and to help him handle his pain.

Harold was too weak to get out of bed now. Shannon spent all her time with him except when she was teaching her French class.

Harold's mind seemed clear, not like her mother's. He liked to tell Shannon of his childhood. His father used to

take him hunting when he was 12 or 13. Once his father started to shoot a beautiful buck. "It was magnificent. We both stood there looking at it and finally my dad put his gun down and let the deer run away. He was too beautiful to kill."

"I remember when I was ten years old and my cousins came to visit and we went fishing together. I didn't like catching the fish so much but I loved the quiet, the beauty of the water and the way the birds seemed to dance on the water, I really felt at home there."

"I remember when my mother used to can tomatoes and green beans and make sauerkraut. She'd make apple pies. We had apples in our own yard. And the whole family would go berry picking and she's make berry pies.

My dad used to take care of the garden and the chickens and gather the eggs.

Harold couldn't urinate although he kept feeling like he needed to. It kept him up all night. He was in pain and afraid.

"Tomorrow we'll ask the nurse to get a catheter," Shannon said. "You'll feel much better."

"They are very uncomfortable. I've had them before. I'd rather have this discomfort."

"It's not a matter of how comfortable it is," Shannon said. "It's how healthy.

If you can't urinate you have to have the catheter to get the toxins out of you. You know that."

The next day Shannon had to teach her French class. It was hard to concentrate on anything besides Harold when he was so ill.

On her lunch hour she decided to stop by the Catholic Church and pray for Harold.

She felt strange walking into the church because she was out of the habit although she had once felt very close to God inside her church. For awhile she even went to Morning Mass every day. But since her beloved husband was killed

and her mother got that awful disease she didn't feel close to God of the church.

"And now you know how much I love Harold. How can you do this to me? I loved you so much and I truly thought that you loved me enough to die for me. If that is true why do you do things that make me want to die?"

She walked up to the altar. She was alone in the church so she spoke out loud to the crucifix. "Why are you doing this to me? When did you stop loving me? I thought you said in the Bible that you would never leave me. And you did. Why did you?" She began crying. "You are love, why did you stop loving me?"

A young priest came out from behind the altar. "Is there anything I can do to help you?" he asked.

"I was just telling God how mad I am."

"I believe God appreciates the fact that you let him know your feelings." The priest said.

"They aren't nice feelings," she said "They are angry, bitter feelings."

"Sometimes we have to hit bottom before we can accept God's healing," the priest said.

"I don't think I can get any deeper," she said. "When do you think He's going to start healing my broken heart?"

"He will help you if you allow it. God never forces himself on anyone. But He will forgive and heal anyone who asks for healing. Sometimes He heals us in a way we do not understand but often we can look back and realize He healed us without our even recognizing it.

"I don't know how to ask," Shannon said.

"Just talk to God like you've been talking to me. In fact, you seemed to be doing a pretty good job of telling him your feelings when I came out of the office."

"I will. Thank you, Father. Sorry I bothered you."

"No bother," he said. "Come back any time."

She looked at her watch, saw that it was time to get back to class so she rushed to school.

After school she went directly to Harold's home. She had been living there ever since she returned to California after visiting her parents. Actually she wasn't living anywhere. She was spending every moment she could with Harold. All of her possessions were still in her home and she was running back and forth to get the things she needed.

While Harold slept, Shannon read his books. She finished the first one and read the other two. He was an excellent writer, sensitive and talented. He was completely honest about his feelings, expressing himself in his writing even more clearly than in his speech. She cried when she read his eternal longing for a home.

Shannon still called her parents frequently and the news was always the same. Everyone's physical health was okay but her mother was sinking deeper and deeper into the never land of Alzheimer's. Shannon longed to see her mother and try to console her but she could not force herself to leave Harold. The doctor had said he could go at any time.

Then one night Harold had a bad fever. He tossed and turned and moaned all night. She wanted to call the doctor but he begged her not to. She prayed hard, "Lord, let him live til morning. I can't watch him die. Watching him die a little at a time is hard enough. But I can't watch him leave me. Please let him live through this night."

When Shannon looked out the window and saw that the sun was rising, she thanked God. Harold had finally fallen asleep. She called Lynda and asked her to spend the day with Harold while she was teaching her French class.

She kissed Harold on the cheek. He was still asleep when she left the house.

Her mind was on Harold all day. She was exhausted and had a hard time concentrating on her French class.

When Shannon returned to Harold's she got a wonderful surprise. Lynda was still there. She ran up to

Shannon. "There's great news. The doctor was here and he says Harold is much better."

"How could he say that? Harold almost died last night."

"Well, go upstairs and look at him." She reached for her purse. "I'm going home I know you can handle things now."

Harold was sitting up in bed reading a book. He smiled when he saw Shannon. "Hello, darling, I'm so glad you're back. I missed you so much."

Shannon could not believe her eyes. His color was back to normal.

She gave him a big hug.

"I thought I was a goner," he said. "Last night was the closest I ever came to goodbye."

"I'm so glad you are better today," she said.

"You had better lie down and take a little nap," he said. "I know I kept you awake last night."

"Maybe a little nap," she said. "Then I want to be up to take advantage of your good health."

She lay down on the sofa in his bedroom covering with his quilt. She thought she would fall asleep right away but she was so excited to see him looking so much better.

She lay there unable to sleep but joyful to know her beloved Harold was better. She forced herself to lie still, pretending to sleep, knowing that he was sitting on his bed reading and watching over her.

After half an hour she got up.

"Are you feeling better/" he asked.

"I had a good rest," she said. "Now I'm going to the kitchen to fix us some supper.

"That's wonderful," he said. "I'm hungry."

That was the first time he'd said he was hungry since he'd been sick in bed.

She was glad she had gone shopping at the Farmer's Market. When she bought the fruits and vegetables, she imagined she would end up throwing most of them away.

She tossed a salad with Romaine lettuce, green pepper, mushroom, cucumber, hard-boiled egg, croutons and cheddar cheese. If Harold ate nothing but salad, he would get plenty of nutrition.

She mashed some potatoes, cooked green beans and baked some Salmon. He had told her that was his favorite fish. She had fresh strawberries and vanilla ice cream for dessert.

She was just getting ready to put everything on a tray and take it to his room when he walked into the kitchen, wearing his gray slacks and light blue cashmere sweater.

"My, don't you look handsome," she said.

"So do you," he said and he kissed her. "Shall we eat at the table for a change?"

"That sounds great," she said.

For the first time since he had been confined to his bed they had dinner on his glass table with a lace tablecloth and fancy napkins. He went to his liquor cabinet and brought out some excellent wine. He put on some romantic music, Frank Sinatra's Love Songs, "All the Way," "Begin the Beguine."

"To your health," she suggested.

"To our love," he said.

"To your health and our love."

Harold was hungry and he managed to eat a decent taste of all the various foods. Shannon thanked God for listening to her cry in the night and letting Harold live longer.

After eating, they held each other and danced in the living room.

Holding each other stirred something deep inside of them. They both started to realize that their relationship wasn't simply an answer to loneliness filling an empty space. It was becoming a very important essence overpowering everything else in their lives.

Then they were both exhausted so they took a nap on his bed, too tired to put on pajamas or take off their clothes.

Shannon fell asleep and dreamed she was back in Europe dancing with the airmen. She was tired and wanted to sit down but each time she sat down Mrs. Kline ordered her to get up and dance so she danced all night and woke up in Harold's arms at 3 a.m.

They got up, put on their pajamas and returned to Harold's bed where they both fell asleep right away and Shannon slept soundly this time without any disturbing dreams.

Harold's health remained good for awhile and he began writing another novel. But every evening when Shannon came home from school he stopped writing to spend time with her.

Shannon had not been able to return to her own writing. She felt a touch of writer's block so she asked Harold for a little help. When she showed him her latest writing, he said, "I can't believe this. We are writing the same book. Why don't we collaborate?"

"That wouldn't be fair to you," she said. "You are a famous writer and I am a beginner. "

"That's not true. You have been keeping a journal and writing short stories and poetry all your life. You are an excellent writer. Remember what I said about how the best writer combines professional experience and amateur enthusiasm. That's what we have together."

Although she felt unworthy of the project the idea of working with him excited her and she readily agreed.

"Most important is the fact that our hearts and souls are united. That is really why I want to write with you."

They wrote spontaneously without an outline or a plan. Sometimes they would sit together by the computer and talk about an idea and then decide what to write. At other times they would each go to the computer alone and pour out their hopes, dreams and intimate thoughts.

On weekends they packed a lunch and had a picnic by the ocean. They rented a boat and went for a ride on a lake. They went to an Indian Casino and spent a day gambling.

They went to a French movie in a theater that showed artistic films.

They celebrated every day they had together both of them aware that it was a miracle that he was still alive.

They made happy memories, filling their days to the brim. Although Shannon usually taught summer classes, she took this summer off to be with Harold. They spent a day at Disneyland, enjoying their many meetings with Mickey Mouse and his friends. Their love turned Disneyland into the magic fantasy land it often is for children. Each little action took on a special meaning. Every light had its own special glow. They chose their entertainment by the length of the lines. Because Harold could not stand in line too long they visited the sites that had the shortest lines. In general his health held up and he was like a child enjoying all the excitement. Harold threw some soft balls at a booth and won a big teddy bear. When he handed it to her, she said, "I so wanted us to have children together. Now we have Harold Jr."

They made each other laugh and found themselves smiling almost all the time when they were together. After dark the magic intensified. The lights glittered. The music seemed more romantic. The crowds happier.

They hugged and kissed like young lovers. They took turns carrying the big teddy bear.

When Shannon was giving the bear a big hug, Harold looked at her with great love and realized what a wonderful mother she would have made..

"I always wanted to be a mother," Shannon said.

"Me too," said Harold. "I always loved kids. I used to be one."

"Me too," she said. "Do you think we will be able to have kids in Heaven?"

"If it's allowed we will," he promised.

They both laughed. "You could never be a mother, Harold but you would have made a great father. Let's ask God for children in Heaven."

"Let's ask him for more time together on earth."

"That is my daily prayer," she said.

"I would love more time," he said. "I love this old earth more every day and it has become so precious to me now that you share it with me. Knowing that my time here is limited makes it even more beautiful. With you by my side I want to live here forever."

"We'll live together as long as we can on this earth and then one day we will join God and love together in Heaven,"

They went to Sea World and sat in the front row and laughed when Shamu splashed them both.

At the wild animal park they entertained each other naming all the animals.

They had a picnic under a beautiful statue of an angel at a cemetery near Harold's home. "I love to spend time in the cemetery," Harold said. "Even when I was a little boy I loved the peace and quiet. I used to pretend the graves were filled with my friends and they were all alive and ready to play with me."

"Were you a lonely child?" she asked.

"Quite the opposite," he said. "I had lots of real people friends of all ages and when they were not around I was surrounded by imaginary friends. I was never lonely."

Shannon wrote in her journal: "We write together now. We have become one person, no longer knowing where one of us ends and the other begins."

She always felt comfortable with Harold. She was never bored when they were together. He made her feel so completely understood, so absolutely loved. Whenever she heard his voice or his laughter she felt alive, aglow. She felt secure with his love. Each day together was an exciting adventure, living in a romantic movie. They read poems, philosophy, and stories to one another Their life together was better than any of the stories.

You always kill the one you love
You can do it with a knife, a gun
Poison Or with a Kiss
A sign, an embrace
And a goodbye
Love can heal
Love can kill
Love can steal
Love can be an angel
Or an evil threat
Love can make your life
A joy or sorrow
Love is a mystery
Only the brave dare try it
Cowards die many times
But only the brave risk
Multiple deaths.

Chapter Eleven
You Always Kill the One You Love

Just when Shannon's life had settled into a loving gratitude for Harold's good health, she got a phone call from her father.

"Shannon, I have terrible news. Your mother has disappeared. Jeanette and I were both in the house and each of us thought the other was with your mother. And she must have just walked away, left the house. Her mind has gotten so bad she does not know your sister Jeanette or me. Most of the time she doesn't even know who she is, doesn't know her own name. She's like a little two year old.

"Can you imagine, Shannon? She's like a little two year old out in the street alone. She left the house this morning and we've been looking for her ever since.

"We didn't want to bother you but now it looks very serious. We called the police and we have everyone we know looking for her."

"I'm glad you called me. I will call the university and get an emergency leave and catch the first plane."

Harold agreed that she must go and help look for her mother.

Leaving Harold was painful. Each morning when she went to work she felt his absence, longed to spend every moment with him. But this time it wasn't quite so painful as it was when she made her last trip to her parents while Harold was deathly ill. Thank God he had lived and was now much healthier even though he was still suffering from AIDS and it was a fatal disease.

She was able to get a plane out the next day. Her sister Jeanette met her at the airport in Columbus. It was a cold October day with a strong wind.

Jeanette threw her arms around Shannon. "Oh, Shannon, I am so glad you have come. Dad and I are so worried. We were always so careful to make certain she was never alone and then when the house was full of people everyone assumed she was being watched and she managed to slip out the door and disappear. We have called everyone. We walked the streets and rode all over town. But Mother is really bad now. She can't even tell her own name let alone where she lives. And she's been gone for a day and a night. Someone should have seen her."

Being back in Columbus made Shannon think of Larry and how much she had loved him. She had been so happy when they were together and so lost without him.

She was thankful for the time they had together. And now she thanked God for putting Harold in her life. She was learning so much about life and literature from him. But why did he have to be so sick?

And why was her mother so sick and so lost? "Lord, please let us find Mother," she prayed.

When they reached her parents' home Shannon took her bags inside and Jeanette made her a ham and cheese sandwich while the coffee boiled. Their father was still out, driving his car up and down all the streets trying to find his wife.

"I don't have much appetite," Shannon said.

"You have to eat something. We haven't been having any meals since Mom got lost but we have to eat a snack from time to time to keep up our energy."

After they ate their sandwiches, Jeanette called the police. "This is Jeanette Johnson again. Have you got any news about my mother, Mrs. Louise Owens?"

The policeman told her, "I'm so sorry, Mam. We are still searching. We have a bulletin out and we have police looking but so far there has been no word, no sign of her. If we learn anything we will call you and if we locate her you can be sure we will bring her home."

Jeanette and Shannon drove to Kinko's where they made some flyers with their Mother's photo. They wrote "Help Us Find Our Mother." Louise Owens suffers from Alzheimer's and wandered out of her home. She lives at 200 East Beaumont Road in Columbus Telephone 614-308-2670 We love her. Please bring her home to us."

A short heavy woman with bright red hair saw the flyers and stopped the girls.

"So you have lost your mother!" she said. "That Alzheimer's is a terrible thing.

"My mother had it also and she used to get lost two or three times a week. Finally for her own sake we had to put her in a nursing home where she got constant care and did not run away anymore."

Another woman, listening to the conversation, joined in, "My Aunt Jenny had Alzheimer's and we had to put her in a home. It was supposed to be very safe with excellent nurses and doctors but she managed to get away from that place. They searched for her for weeks.. It was in the winter with blizzards and snow everywhere and she wasn't even wearing a coat.

"They found her in the woods, frozen to death."

Shannon and Jeanette both gasped. "How awful."

"Oh, I didn't mean to upset you girls anymore than you are but it is the truth and you really do need to know the facts."

The two sisters began to walk down all the streets in their neighborhood calling their mother's name. "We have already knocked on the doors of all of the neighbors we know. Now we have to begin knocking on stranger's doors. We are not going to give up until we find her."

They knocked on the door of a cute little brick house. When the owner opened the door Shannon was surprised to see Mrs. Klinker, her high school Latin teacher. Her hair was white and her skin was wrinkled but she had retained the bright blue eyes and wholesome smile.

"Is that you, Shannon?" she asked.

"Yes, Mrs. Klinker. I've been traveling since I saw you last but I came back home because my mother is missing and we're looking for her."

"Yes, I ran into your mother once when she had slipped away from home. I asked her her name and she said she had misplaced it. I asked her where she lived and she said, 'In the white house with the blue shingles.' By that time I recognized her and took her home. Your father was out looking for her so I sat there with her on the porch swing until he returned.

" I'm so sorry she is missing and so sorry she is so ill."

"Are you going to be in Columbus very long? I'd love to get together and hear about what you have been doing with yourself."

"My plans are all up in the air at the moment but I would love to get together and have a nice visit with you when Mom is home and we can all relax."

They left some flyers with Mrs Klinker to give to her family and friends.

As they walked a little farther they ran into Larry's sister Loretta who had been shopping and was carrying several large bags. "Shannon, how wonderful to see you! I had no idea you were in town!"

"It was very sudden," she explained. "My Mother has Alzheimer's as you know and she left the house alone and we are all terrified. She has been gone for a day and a night and no one has seen her."

"Oh, I am so sorry. Let me put my bags in the house and maybe I can help you search."

"The biggest help would be if you could get on the phone and call everyone you know and see if anyone has seen her. And you could take some flyers to give to anyone that is interested."

"I'll take those flyers and I will be glad to make those calls," she said. "Hope to see you again before you go back to California. I will pray you find her."

When they arrived at St. Joseph Catholic Church, they went to the rectory looking for Father O'Conner.

"Hello," Father said. "It's good to see some of my favorite parishioners. Shannon, are you back in Columbus for good?"

"No, Father, something terrible has happened. Mother wandered out of the house and got lost. She has been gone for a night and a day. We need all the prayers we can get."

"I'll be happy to pray for her. I will offer my Mass for her in the morning. You two may want to attend but if you are out searching for her that is okay too.

"And I will give you the phone number for the Church's Prayer Line. Call them and they will get some real prayer warriors working on the case. Let's say a little prayer right now."

Together they said the Lord's Prayer, a Hail Mary and Glory be to God and asked God to bless Louise and hold her close, keep her safe and return her to her family.

They left some flyers with Father O'Conner who put one up at the entrance of the church and left a stack near the door.

When they were exhausted, the two women went home. Jeanette called all the hospitals in their area and when there was no sign of their mother she reluctantly called the morgue.

"We only have one Jane Doe. She is too young to be your mother. She is about 19 and it appears she died of an overdose of drugs."

"Every one else has been identified. Does your mother have any identification on her?"

"No," Jeanette said. When she hung up the phone she said, "When we find Mother we have to make sure she always has identification on her."

Jeanette put on some coffee and a short time later their father came in looking like a drowned rat, completely exhausted and depressed. He smiled when he saw Shannon and hurried to put his arms around her. "Shannon, I am so glad you came home."

Jeanette turned on the television just in time to catch the news. They were all shocked but pleased when the news announced said, "A 70 year old Columbus woman is missing and her family is desperately asking for your help to find the woman. Louise Owens suffers from Alzheimer's and has completely lost her memory so she will need help finding her way home."

"I hope that news program helps us get Mom back home."

The phone rang and Jeanette answered.

"Hello, is this the home of Mrs. Louise Owens?"

"Yes, I am her daughter Jeanette."

The woman took a deep breath. "I am so sorry to tell you this but your mother is dead. She walked right into my car. I didn't see her at all until she was there on the front of my car. I don't understand how it happened. I drove her to the hospital but she had died by the time we got there."

Jeanette called the hospital and made arrangements to have her mother's body moved to the mortuary near the church. She called Father O'Conner and made plans for the funeral.

Shannon called Harold and told him the sad news.

"Do you want me to come for the funeral?" he asked.

"I would love to see you," she told him. "But I don't think all that traveling will be good for your health. You just stay home and take good care of yourself so you can entertain and inspire me when I get home."

"I am really lonely without you." he said.

"Me too." She said.

"I am so sorry about your mother," he said.

"Yes, me too."

All the family and close friends gathered in Shannon's parents' home for her mother's wake. They were celebrating her birthday in Heaven, the day she died.

Her mother was wearing her favorite dress, a pink satin gown with white lace. Shannon remembered how her mother had consoled her when her grandmother died.

"She will sleep forever but her soul will be happy in Heaven with Jesus and his mother."

They played Irish tunes, especially "Danny Boy" which was Louise's favorite. And "I will take you home, Kathleen."

Everyone brought food and the kitchen was loaded with various delicious dishes.

There was meat loaf, baked potatoes, deviled eggs, scalped potatoes, corn beef and cabbage, various salads, apple pie, cherry pie, lemon meringue, chocolate cake and more. They all ate and drank and told stories of the good old days with Louise before she got sick. They were drinking whiskey, wine, beer, rum, vodka and soda.

Most of the adults were getting high, some were actually drunk but they kept partying until they fell asleep in the chairs and sofa right where they were.

The funeral took place at St. Joseph's Church. Father O'Conner said the Mass.

When the mourners were at the church entrance those people already inside turned to face them. The priest began the prayers. "Praised be God, the Father of Our Lord Jesus Christ, the Father of Mercies, and the God of all Consolations. He comforts us in all our afflictions and enables us to comfort those in trouble with the same consolation we have received from Him."

Shannon could feel the tears falling down her face. She wanted to pretend they were not there but she finally took a hanky and wiped them.

When it was time for Communion her father, Jeanette and Shannon all took the Host and drank the wine, the body and blood of Jesus Christ. "Jesus, please help us get through this terrible loss," Shannon prayed. "And take care of my beloved Harold."

The choir began to sing "Let There Be Peace on Earth" and Shannon felt a little more peace in her own soul.

Each time Shannon looked at the coffin she felt the tears begin.

As the service ended everyone prayed "May the angels lead you into Paradise. May the martyrs come to welcome you and take you to the holy city, the new and eternal Jerusalem."

After Mass they all returned to the house where they had even more food than at the Wake. Shannon put a chicken breast, some mashed potatoes, green beans, a lettuce

and tomato salad on the table before her. She had no appetite but she tried to eat a little taste of everything on her plate. For desert she had apple pie and as she tried to eat it she remembered the wonderful apple pies her mother used to make. She would never taste them again. The tears ran down her face once more.

Shannon tried to speak with all the guests but she found it difficult to carry on a conversation.

The closest she came to a conversation was with her father "I will really miss your mother," he said, "But I have been missing her for a long time. She hasn't really been with us since she got this awful disease that robbed her of her mind. It was harder on me losing her mind and her spirit to the disease than it was losing her body to death. That was just the final curtain but the play ended long ago."

That night Shannon called Harold and told him of her day.

"I miss you so much," Harold said, "but I want you to stay with your father as long as he needs you. It will be hard for him to be alone. After you've been caring for someone you love and have put all of your thoughts and strength and mind into caring for them you are empty when they are gone."

"I'm sure you are right," she said. "I will spend some time with my dad but I am so eager to be with you."

"We will be together soon," he promised.

You can't pay anyone to sing
A lullaby with all their heart.
Anyone can sing a lullaby
If he or she
Has a heart.
Enjoy your life
So you can
Enjoy your death.

Chapter Twelve
Lullaby

Shannon knew that her father would never be ready to let her go. He had never lived alone and did not want to start now. But at least he had Jeanette and Frank living in the same town and paying lots of attention to him.

Shannon would not have minded staying with her father indefinitely if it had not been for Harold alone waiting for her and for her job teaching French at the University.

Saying goodbye to Jeanette and their father was difficult. The two of them took her to the airport and stayed with her until the last possible moment when she had to enter the security section where she had to go alone. They clung to each other for a last minute hug and then she turned and started toward her plane.

The plane ride was smooth. Shannon read awhile and then took a nap. When she arrived in San Diego, she began searching for Harold. She found him at the baggage section.

They ran into each other's arms and held on as though they might lose each other if they let go.

Shannon was so happy to be back with the man she loved that she just wanted to sit and hold him and feel his arms around her. Knowing that he had a fatal disease that was contagious and easily spread during sex she hadn't felt tempted to make love before. Now she wanted to be as close to her beloved as possible. They could use protection and take their chances.

But Harold said no. "After I am dead, you will be the only part of me that lives on.

"You must stay alive for my sake as well as yours. We must not take any chance. You know I want you as much as you want me but we can't. There is no discussing it."

Silent tears slipped down her face. He wiped them off.

They sat in front of the fireplace where Harold had built a fire which was not needed because the weather was still warm in California but he found it romantic.

"I'm so sorry about your mother," Harold said.

"It is sad. Funerals are always sad but Mother's mind had died quit a while ago and that was really the saddest part."

"Shannon, do you believe in Heaven? What do you think happens to us when we die?"

"Sometimes I don't even know if I believe in immortality." She pushed her long auburn hair out of her face. "At other times I'm very religious, a good Christian; secure in God's love, certain a Heaven is waiting."

"What is Heaven like, how do you see it? He asked.

"I'm certain it's magnificent, much more exciting and beautiful than people imagine it. I think it's a big surprise that God saves for us."

"We all have doubts at times," he said. "Even great saints. St. John of the Cross called it the dark night of the soul."

"I have had my share of dark nights," she said, 'But then I've had so many beautiful days I can't complain. I love life."

"Since I got sick I came to see how beautiful life is. Knowing it's so fragile I have come to appreciate it in a way most people never do."

"I remember my mother once told me she thought the more people we loved in Heaven, the easier it was to join them. She said, "I think when it's our time to die all the souls on earth who love us try to hold us here, like a big tug o war and all the people in Heaven try to bring us up to join them."

The next morning the sun was bright. The sky was blue with tiny fluffy white clouds. There was a soft breeze and neither of them felt any lack in their life at the moment. Both refused to think of Harold's health problem.

Something inside gave each of them hope that the healing power of love would solve that problem.

Shannon had fixed a picnic lunch and Harold took her to his favorite cemetery. It covered several acres of well cared for land with rich green grass, majestic trees, and neatly trimmed bushes. Red, orange and yellow flowers grew over many of the graves. Some plots had beautiful statues of angels or Jesus or life-sized stone people. Every gravestone seemed to have its own personality.

"I used to play here with my friends when I was a little boy," he said.

They sat under Harold's favorite angel and Shannon spread out a table cloth and laid out the food. She had fried chicken, a lettuce salad, bananas, apples, grapes, orange juice and bottled water. She had made chocolate chip cookies for dessert.

"I do like cemeteries," Shannon said. "They are so peaceful and they usually have a fantastic view. I am so glad that we can appreciate it."

After lunch they lay in each other's arms admiring the crowds and enjoying each other's presence.

"Harold, would you like to marry me?" she asked, surprising herself as much as she surprised him.

"I would love to marry you, Shannon, if only we could really be together, to be free together, to make love and enjoy one another completely but you know I can't. I love you too much to risk your life."

"It's okay," she said. "We can continue our life the way it is but I want us to really belong to one another. I want the world to know that we are together."

"I'm sure it would make my mother and dad happy," he said.

So it was decided.

They called the priest that Shannon had spoken with earlier and he agreed to perform the ceremony if they would take the Pre-Nuptial classes.

"Are you going to invite your parents? " Shannon asked.

"I would rather not," Harold said. "They aren't much fun."

"I wish you would," she said. "It would make the wedding seem complete with both of our families."

Harold called his parents and invited them to the wedding. They did not seem very happy but they did agree to come.

"I haven't seen them for years," Harold said. "I was so upset because they were so mean to all my friends."

"I hope they will like me," Shannon said.

"Everyone likes you, Shannon."

Shannon called Jeanette and Frank and her father. They arrived a few days before the wedding so Jeanette could help Shannon choose her outfit and help her prepare the way Shannon had helped Jeanette prepare for her own wedding. Jeanette and Shannon's friend Lynda were her bride's maids. They wore light blue gowns. Jeanette, Frank and their father stayed at Shannon's apartment and she stayed there with them, going back and forth to Harold's.

When Harold's parents arrived they did not look too happy. Shannon couldn't believe how cold they were to him. His father shook his hand and his mother put her arms around him stiffly and quickly removed them. They knew he had a fatal disease and they might never see him again. They had not seen him for years and yet they showed no love. Shannon wondered if she had made a mistake asking Harold to invite them. She was afraid they would mistreat him. They insisted on staying in a hotel.

Harold asked John Stutzer, a history teacher at the university, to be his best man. Shannon had known John at school but this was the first time she had spent any time with him outside of work. She found him a delightful new friend.

Their wedding day arrived. The sun was shining. The sky was a clear blue with a slight breeze.

Shannon felt graceful in her pale pink wedding gown with white lace. She had never seen Harold looking so handsome. He wore his grey suit with a lighter gray shirt and tie. She felt they made a great couple. She hoped they would always be happy together and she prayed that his health would improve. Shannon and Jeanette had decorated the church with roses, lilies and daffodils.

A small reception was held in the church hall. There was a live band and the place was decorated with multicolored flowers and streamers. The first music was romantic and then lively. Shannon and Harold danced the first dance. Then Jeanette and Frank and Lynda and John joined them. Harold's parents danced one dance and then sat down for the rest of the evening. Shannon, Jeanette and Lynda took turns dancing with John, Harold and Jeanette's father.

Jeanette and Frank still looked happy together. Harold and Shannon fed each other cake and deliberately spread the cake and icing all over each other.

When they finished eating, they opened the last bottle of champagne and John and Jeanette toasted the bride and groom.

Shannon threw her bouquet into her friend Lynda's arms. Lynda held the flowers up for everyone to see.

As soon as they were alone, Harold and Shannon threw their arms around each other and drew as close together as they could manage. Their love was intensified by the knowledge that their time together was severely limited.

They whispered each other's name over and over and clung to one another. He covered her body with his kisses. Their kisses and touches were gentle and loving at first, tender and soft, but they grew in intensity and desperation.

Harold stopped the passionate embrace before they went too far. "I want you so much, my darling, but we can not take a chance. You are all that I will leave to represent me on earth when I go and I want you healthy and beautiful like you are right now."

"Let's never be careless with our love," she said. "Let's always love each other the way we do now."

"I promise to love you even more than I love you now although I don't know how that will be possible."

"You're a poet, Harold," she said.

"That is because you are my inspiration. You would make a poet out of any man."

"You're the only man I ever want."

"I couldn't share you with anyone."

Before Shannon's father, Jeanette and Frank returned to Ohio they helped Shannon prepare all of her possessions for the movers who brought them to Harold's house. She gave up her apartment and moved in with him. Although she had been spending most of her time in his home she really felt they were together now that they only had one home.

For the most part, their honeymoon was spent in each other's arms, just lying together sharing their lives and their love.

They shared little humiliations and misunderstandings they had never been able to tell another person. They each

dug back as far as their memories would go and attempted to share their entire lives.

Harold told her how his father had great difficulty supporting his family as a professor in a small college town. The problem was intensified by the fact that his father was an addicted gambler betting on horses, games and anything else he could find to bet on. Harold was told as a child he should never speak about his family to strangers and he never had. Of course Shannon was not a stranger. She was his closest family so he felt free to tell her everything. It was a liberating feeling.

"My father was my hero," Harold said. "I looked up to him. He was a champion tennis player and a champion swimmer and all the neighborhood kids admired him. He enjoyed spending time with us kids, showed real interest in everything we did, encouraged us in our ventures and made us feel loved and special.

"But once I finally told my father I was gay, he said, "I forbid it. You are not gay. You are my son and you will find a nice girl and marry her and have grandchildren for your mother and me."

"When I told him that was impossible. I could not help being the way I was, feeling the way I did, he got angry and told me to get out of his house and never return until I had come to my senses"

"I'm so sorry you had to go through that," she said.

One day Shannon asked Harold, "Do you believe in Reincarnation? Do you believe there is a chance that we've been together before or that we'll be together on earth again?"

"I feel we've always been together in spirit and that we always will be. I don't think it really matters whether it's on this earth, in Heaven or in any other place. The important thing is our love, our now."

"I've thought about Reincarnation," she said. "I know many people believe in it and I can't say they are wrong.

But we Catholics have Purgatory so we can finish up things after we die and we don't have to come back again."

Shannon began to feel so at ease around Harold she didn't feel she had to pretend around him, not that she ever did but she realized she had always tried to show him her best side, to pretend to be happier than she was on a day when she felt depressed or upset about something. Now she allowed herself to show exactly what she felt.

He did not seem to love her any the less for it. In fact, if anything, his love was constantly growing.

It was a beautiful November day in San Diego. A bright warm sun lit up the earth and a fresh soothing breeze made certain no one got too warm. Most of the trees still had their green leaves but a few had changed colors for autumn showing orange, yellow, red and brown. The palm trees stood proud.

They loved to drive to the ocean and sit on a bench and meditate on the water.

The clouds were drifting and forming all sorts of interesting shapes. Shannon found herself hypnotized and unable to look at anything else except for her occasional glances at her beloved Harold and each glance made her heart leap even after two intensive months of marriage.

"What will your life be like after I'm gone? Harold asked.

"I don't want to think about it," she said.

"Shannon, you have to understand. We both know I don't have long to live and we need to prepare for it. We've been blessed with this remission. It really is a gift from God, a thank you probably for so many prayers.

"I need to talk about death at times. I know it's not far away. Whenever I bring up the subject everyone stops me. My doctors won't even talk about it. They change the subject."

"If it helps you to talk about death, Harold, of course I will talk with you. If you have to die soon, I thank God for letting me be with you when it happens."

"Well I have to admit that after my love for you, my death is the most important thing on my mind these days. I can't pretend I'm going to live forever or for a long time. I want to be ready when the time comes. I don't want it to sneak up on me. I don't want it to be a big surprise for either one of us. I want us to be prepared and to welcome Mr. Death graciously. I want to think of death as a natural part of life. I've been around many deaths recently and I thought I had come to accept death as natural. I thought I was used to it. I didn't think it would upset me much when it was my time to go. But I guess it is hard for anyone to accept their own death nonchalantly. And since you came into my life my life has become much more precious and death so much harder to accept."

"I know what you mean," Shannon said, "It's so hard for me to accept your death. I love you so much. I want you here with me forever."

They clung to each other. A refreshing breeze raised the edge of her skirt and she reached to pull it over her legs.

"What do you think it's like after we die, Harold?"

" I hope Heaven is similar to earth. Look around you. I don't know how any place could be more beautiful. The trouble is on earth we are too busy or too anxious to appreciate this beauty. I hope Heaven will give us time to take in all the awesome beauty."

"I haven't thought too much about what Heaven is like although I have thought quite a bit on what we must do or be to get into Heaven." Shannon said.

"I figure Jesus will be there to meet us or he will send a guardian angel. But we will definitely get to spend time with Jesus and enjoy his love. And our close family and friends who are already there will come to help us feel at home. They will show us around and get us settled up there. And then I guess it will be a lot like earth without the hassle."

"The only thing that bothers me about Heaven is what will I do up there until you join me?"

"Don't worry about that," she said. "One hundred years on earth is like a second in Heaven where eternity is the time limit so even though it might seem like a long time to me it won't be any time to you until I'm sitting on a cloud beside you."

"I'll miss you an eternity's worth in those few minutes," he said. "It has seemed an eternity each time you went to Ohio."

"I know what you mean, Harold. Any time we are apart it's too long.

"I miss you any time you go to the bathroom," she said, laughing.

"I am so glad we found each other. You are the best thing that ever happened to me."

"I feel the same way about you," he said, "Of course it would be easier for me to die if I didn't have you to leave. But this time together is worth any extra pain it causes me. I love you so much."

"I know, Harold, I love you the same way."

They shared their lunch with the squirrels and pigeons leaving some bread crumbs for the birds who refused to join them as they ate.

From the start our love was boundless.
Free spirits with all consuming love.
Our light lit up our world
heart and soul
until death shattered it.
love was romantic and tragic
but the glow never ends.
Our love like our heart goes on.

Chapter Thirteen
Our Heart Goes On

"One of the things I love most about you, Harold, is your wonderful listening ear." Shannon said as she sat in Harold's back yard swing. "I feel like I can talk about anything and you will understand and help me to understand. Sometimes you even talk about death like it's an old friend."

"I'd never call death an old friend. He's more like a relative that keeps showing up on your doorstep, always causing trouble but because he's family you have to take him in."

"At least you aren't terrified of him. I always have been so afraid I wouldn't even talk about him"

The swing made a loud squeak and Harold promised himself he'd oil it in the future.

"Shannon, I am so glad you are just the way you are. Ever since I learned I was actively in the process of dying I can't stand to be around phony people. You are for real and

I love you for it. I can't afford to waste my time on phoniness. I have to be able to say what I mean. I don't have time for pretending. I am extra-sensitive to pretence now. When I am around many people I want to shake them and shout, "Please stop playing games with yourself. Be real. Stop acting and just be."

"I know what you mean. I love to be around real people. That's why I love you so much."

No matter what they talked about, they always ended up in one another's arms expressing their great love.

One morning Harold asked Shannon to go to the graveyard with him to pick out his plot.

"Do you have a special one in mind?" she asked.

"No," he said. All of my dead family members that I know of are buried in Massachusetts. But I'd rather be here in California where I knew you. I want to be cremated. Then it won't be so difficult moving me around."

"If you want to be buried in Massachusetts I would be happy to see that it was done as you wanted it."

"I'd like to make the arrangements while we are here," he said.

They went to the office and a sales clerk escorted them to the plots that were available. He tried not to show his impatience as they went from place to place, checking out the view, the neighborhood and the freshness of the grass.

They chose joining plots on the hill where they had enjoyed their picnic shortly after they met. Then they chose their headstones, simple, identical marble stones with their names, date of birth, and date of death to be added and beloved spouse.

"Now let's choose the urn for my ashes.

"Do we have to?" she asked.

"Wouldn't it be easier if we did it together than if you had to do it all alone?"

"You are so thoughtful, my darling. You are right."

"I woke up this morning thinking of all the work my death will make for you and I decided to help you out."

"That's what I call a thoughtful husband. The only thing I would like better is a husband who would never die and leave me."

"You know I will be waiting for you in Heaven."

Harold chose a navy blue urn with silver trim.

"And what will you do, my love, after I am gone?"

"Miss you like hell. In addition, I will write every day in your honor and live as fully as I can because I will be living for two. I once heard death described as an ever-changing sea. We are all part of that sea. Each of us is a wave. We come and go but the sea goes on. It is always there."

"You can talk about the sea or talk about God. We are all a part of God and whether we live or die we remain a part of Him. So when we stay close to God we stay close to one another." Harold laughed. "Shannon, I didn't know if I believed in God and you have me preaching about him."

They went into a book store and Shannon found a lovely poster showing a beautiful butterfly resting on some colorful flowers. It read: "What the caterpillar thinks is the end of life the butterfly knows is the beginning." They bought it for their bedroom.

The next morning golden sunlight came streaming through their bedroom windows. Shannon opened her eyes and looked at Harold sleeping beside her, his arm over her stomach. His natural beauty made her heart dance. The knowledge that he would not be with her much longer tore at her insides.

He looked so peaceful lying there, his face relaxed and his curls surrounded his head like a halo. She leaned over and lightly kissed his lips. He mumbled something and opened his eyes.

He reached up for her and she bent down to kiss him.

He held her loving, kissed her gently, then said, "Could you help me up. I have to go to the bathroom."

She helped him out of bed and noticed he was dizzy as he found his balance and walked into the bathroom with such grace you would never know he had been dizzy a few minutes earlier.

Shannon was looking out the bedroom window noticing that even in California there were autumn leaves on some trees and watching the wind urge the leaves to come away. Harold screamed and fell. The sound cut right through her.

She ran down the hall, threw open the door and found Harold lying unconscious on the bathroom floor.

She called an ambulance and was told not to move his body so she sat on the bathroom floor next to him, longing to touch him but afraid she might do him harm.

After what seemed hours, but according to her watch was fifteen minutes, the ambulance pulled up in front of the house.

Shannon rode in the front of the ambulance taking Harold to the University hospital. She stayed in the waiting room while the doctors examined him.

After an interminable wait, Shannon saw a doctor approaching.

"We are going to have to admit him," he said. There's something wrong with his back. He hurt it when he fell. Since he is suffering from AIDS we must be very careful that there is no infection. His immune system is gone. Whatever is happening to him is very serious. He's conscious now and he's in great pain."

"Can I see him?"

"In a few minutes. We want to give him something for the pain first. Then he will probably go right to sleep but you can spend a few minutes with him if you wish."

Shannon thought he was unconscious when she entered the room. He was lying so still. Then she heard him moan. The sound went right through her.

She walked closer to him. "Harold, darling, are you okay?"

"Shannon, I love you. I am not okay. I hurt. My back is killing me. I've never hurt like this before. Don't leave me, Shannon. Stay with me please."

"I won't leave you, Harold. I will never leave you. I'll be right here. If they kick me out of the room I will wait outside the door until I can see you again."

"This pain is unbearable, Shannon. Could you ask the nurses to give me something for the pain?"

She hurried to the nearest nurse. "My husband is in terrible pain. Can you help him?"

"We just gave him a very powerful shot. It hasn't started working yet. It will start any minute now."

"He's in great pain."

When she returned to Harold's room, he was sleeping soundly. She waited at the chair next to the bed. It was painful for her because he kept moaning in his sleep.

Several times she asked the nurse if there wasn't something else she could do for him because he was moaning and must be in pain even though he was asleep.

The nurse said, "If he is asleep he could not really be suffering too much."

"Then why is he moaning?" she asked.

"I don't know why he is moaning but I do know that the shot we gave him was powerful enough to put him to sleep so it must be powerful enough to stop the pain."

They kept Harold in the hospital for a week trying to figure out what exactly was wrong with his back. At first they thought it was related to a fall from a horse when he was a teenager. But further research seemed to show that it was not related to any earlier injury.

The doctors would not allow him to go home because he was in too much pain and they didn't think he could control the pain at home.

Harold slept most of the time and when he was awake he struggled to keep from shouting about the pain.

Faithful to her promise to Harold, Shannon did not leave the hospital. She remained in his room as long as she could. The nurses allowed her to stay there even at night. When they asked her to leave for a short time while they did a procedure she would go out to the cafeteria for coffee or a

snack. She was always at the door when the nurses were ready to allow her to enter his room again.

The doctors and nurses began to worry about Shannon. They begged her to go home and get some rest but she refused.

Then one day a doctor came to talk with Shannon, "I'm so sorry but I have very bad news. The AIDS is attacking his body again.

The doctors hadn't told Harold the bad news yet but Shannon knew he would want to know. She forced herself to tell him.

"I'm sorry," he said. "But we both knew this time was coming. Don't ever forget we have a date in Heaven. I will be waiting for you with bated breath."

Shannon sat by the bed, praying that God would ease his physical pain as well as the mental pain.

But he suddenly hit the side of the bed with all his power. The force was so strong his fist began bleeding. She called the nurse to wash his hand.

"Well, Shannon, I may not be coming home anymore. I never imagined it would end so soon. I thought I was going earlier but then when I got better I was sure I would have more time with you." She was convinced he could live longer if he wanted to.

Shannon continued to hang around the hospital but she noticed a change in Harold. He was no longer struggling to get well. He had accepted the idea that death was here, waiting patiently in the outskirts. Whenever death decided to make his entry, Harold was prepared to accompany him.

Shannon didn't want to think about it. She was convinced he could live longer if he wanted to.

Shannon decided to take the doctors' advice and go home and rest a bit. "Get some sleep, Mrs. Dunlap. You've been here over a week without a good night's sleep. If you don't get some rest we will be treating Harold in one room and you in another."

Passing St. Joseph's Church Shannon decided to stop for a prayer. A funeral service was going on. It must be someone important she thought because there was a large crowd. The church was beautifully decorated with magnificent floral arrangements, lighted candles and a banner around the top of the Altar proclaiming that Christ is the Resurrection.

A choir of young adults was singing "Amazing Grace" with sorrowful beauty. When the choir finished their song, the Bishop stood up to talk. "We are all stunned by the death of a young man that all of America considered a friend. He entertained us with his music. He collected money for those in need anywhere. Looking at the wonderful things he was able to accomplish in his short life, we wonder why God didn't give him more years on this earth.

"Perhaps such deaths are meant to remind us that no one knows how long we will live and we must put our trust in God, the One who knows everything. He created us for a purpose. He has counted every hair on our heads. He has numbered all of our days. He knows when we will be called home. We cannot change that and we should not try.

"When we pray the Our Father, we say thy will be done. Let us pray to love God's will. And today we pray to be able to accept God's will. We will never know God's reason for calling Danny O'Shea home. Let us thank God for the short time we had with him and all the beauty and love he brought to this earth."

The choir began singing "How Great Thou Art." Shannon left the church, feeling she had just had an intense conversation with God.

Shannon went home and took a leisurely bubble bath and then lay on her bed, thought about how much she missed Harold, She put Harold Jr, the teddy bear he had won for her, in bed and fell asleep after one week without any good rest.

When Shannon got to the hospital the next day the nurses said, "Your husband has been asking for you,"

She hurried into his room. Harold looked weak and pale the way he had looked before when he was close to death.

"Shannon, darling. I missed you," he said. His voice was weak.

"I missed you too."

In a short time, Harold was shouting with pain. The nurse gave him an injection and he passed out right away. He was moaning and sweating and his hair was wet. He woke up and she told him she had to step outside because it was killing her to watch him suffer.

"Do you want to trade places?" he asked.

"I would be willing if you could arrange it."

He squeezed her hand, "I've never known any greater happiness in my life than I have known with you. You have made my dying days worth living. Thank you, my love."

When the doctors admitted that Harold was dying and could be gone any time, she begged to take him home to die. They refused saying he was in too much pain and needed to be in the hospital where they could control the level of pain.

Shannon reached out and took Harold's hand. She was suddenly aware of how alive he was at that moment, of the greatness of the life force within his wasted, distorted body. He was as alive as Shannon was. How could death be so near to him?

She tried to remind herself that he would be gone soon, leaving her and his pain far behind. She must try to be relieved and happy for him. But how could she ever face the loss, fill the empty void that he would leave in her?

One day soon his rhythmic breathing would cease and his spirit would slip out of his already decaying body. He had surrendered to death and was ready to accompany him.

She knew for certain that on her own death bed she would call out his name.

Once she slipped out of her body he would be there to welcome her home.

After Harold died, Shannon wrote in her journal:.

"Our love was strong enough to stop the world but not strong enough to keep death away. I will always treasure the memories we shared, memories of Heaven.

"As much as it hurt to lose him, I will never regret loving him. Our love was precious. Our love changed me forever. Dancing to silent music, we felt bliss that lingers long after the beloved is gone. A part of him will stay with me forever."

We gave ourselves completely
to love.
Remembering happiness.
Together.
It was a magic time
the world was young.
my memory.
We were One
Growing up together.
Losing him
I am half a person until
His smile, his hands, his eyes
speak to me
across the ages, eternal spaces,
and I know the enduring power of love.

Chapter Fourteen
A Magic Time

After Harold died, Shannon felt as though she were half a person.

She forced herself to go back to work teaching French at the University but she felt like a robot as she taught her class.

Each night she would rush home to the beautiful house that her beloved Harold had left her. In the beginning she

did nothing but cry. Then she began describing her pain in her diary.

Her friend Lynda would stop by from time to time. But when she tried to get Shannon to go some place with her Shannon always refused.

Then she remembered the book that she and Harold were writing together and she started writing where the two of them had left off. As she wrote she felt him leaning over her shoulder, shaking his head in approval or in disagreement.

It made her feel close to him so she spent as much time as she could arrange at her computer writing.

She could hear him as he spoke in writing class, "It is quality and not quantity that matters in your work. We can't do everything but if we try we can do something. Let us celebrate every miracle in our lives."

One day after several months of work, she came to the end of the book that she and Harold started together. She called his agent, Alice Foster and told her about the book.

"Harold mentioned that book to me several months before he died but I had no idea you were finishing it. Send it to me right away."

Shannon went over every word, careful to correct any faults. Then she printed it up and put it in the mail.

Once she had mailed the book, she felt lost with nothing to do but teach her French class.

She sat down at her computer and waited for a message from Harold with a new book to write. He had won a Pulitzer Prize for his powerful book on Home. In fact, he had written three books on the subject so she decided to write of the homes in her life and she realized that all of them had received their meaning from the love that surrounded them, the people she loved who loved her and helped her create a home. Now she lived alone but Harold had filled the house with his love and she could feel it in every room.

Three months after Alice, the agent had received the book she called to say, "Shannon. I have good news,

Harold's old publisher, Random House wants to publish this one. They're calling it DESTINATIONS by Harold and Shannon Dunlap. And they want to send you on a book tour."

"But I have my French class to teach."

"Take a leave. They are willing to spend a lot of money on Harold's last book. Do it for Harold."

The University staff was impressed by her success and they willingly gave her the leave.

Nine months later, by pretending Harold was with her she was able to put up with the many plane trips, the nights in hotels and days in book stores signing books, being interviewed on television and radio.

Alice kept in close touch, calling her every few days to find out if everything was all right and if she needed anything.

Each place she went had a representative of the publisher or of the bookstores in that town to entertain her so she didn't get lonely except for the eternal loneliness she felt for Harold.

One night Alice called with great news. "Shannon, the book is on the New York Times Best Seller list."

When Shannon arrived in Columbus, Ohio, her sister Jeanette and her father met her at the airport. They had a meal together and then drove her to the Barnes & Noble bookstore where she was to sign books. Her family begged her to move back to Ohio. "You are all alone there in California. Please come and live near us."

"I love Ohio and I will always feel at home here but Harold left me a beautiful house in California and I feel close to him there so I can never leave."

Alice called to say DESTINATIONS was number two on the Best Seller list. And after another month it was number one.

Alice returned home and continued working on her next book

She called it ALL THE DOGS IN EUROPE BARK. She wrote about the peacetime Air Force in France. The book moved rapidly as she remembered her days in the service club. Alice handled this book also and sold it to Simon and Schuster. They too asked her to go on a book tour. It was summer and Lynda was free as neither of them was teaching so Lynda accompanied her. She enjoyed it much more with her friend along.

ALL THE DOGS IN EUROPE BARK made the New York Times bestseller list but it never made first or second. Shannon was satisfied.

She was making enough money that she did not have to keep teaching French unless she wanted to. Any way, Harold had left her a good sum of money and his beautiful house.

Then one evening when she was taking her walk she looked around her and everything looked different. She did not recognize any of the streets. She was terrified having no idea what was happening. Then she remembered how her mother acted when she had Alzheimer's and she was even more terrified.

She wandered the streets unable to remember her own address and unable to recognize all the streets that were near her home. When she finally found the house, she ran inside and shut the door. Home at last. From that day she was afraid to go outside alone.

She started working on her next book. She would be writing along fine with no problem and then she would forget a common word.

She went into the kitchen to heat up some soup but she forgot how to use the can opener. She sat down on the floor and cried.

When her friend Lynda came to visit, Shannon told her what had been happening. "My mother had Alzheimer's. I'm afraid I am getting it."

Lynda took her to her doctor who examined her and said, "It does look like Alzheimer's." He prescribed some medicine and suggested she get a live-in companion.

The doctor told her she should not drive a car as long as she was having these spells.

Lynda brought Anita, a young Mexican girl to help take care of Shannon. Anita had a five-year-old daughter Monica. They lived with Anita's mother in San Diego.

Shannon liked Anita from the beginning. She was a happy young lady, who smiled most of the time. She loved to sing. She was a hard worker who kept the house immaculate, was a good cook and liked to play dominos, cards and made up games. She took good care of Shannon, making sure she ate nutritious food and took her walk each day.

They went to movies together. Anita showed her pictures of her daughter Monica and promised to bring Monica to meet her one of these days.

They went on picnics by the ocean and tested various restaurants.

Anita started teaching Shannon Spanish and Shannon was teaching her English.

Then one day the Santa Ana winds blew into San Diego starting fires all over. At first Shannon and Anita paid no attention to the News but then there was an announcement that everyone on their street was being asked to evacuate.

Anita helped Shannon to pack a small suitcase being careful to include her medicine and several changes of clothes and a night gown and robe and slippers.

Anita drove Shannon's car to her Grandma's house where she and her daughter lived.

Grandma Salud's home was a neat little white house with three bedrooms. The front yard was covered with beautiful flowers, jasmine, yellow, red, orange, peach and white roses, lilacs, and honeysuckle.

The furniture was plain, neat and clean, a beige sofa with two matching arm chairs. A beige carpet covered the

floor. Cheerful pictures decorated the wall. There was a television set on a table.

Grandma Salud welcomed Shannon with a smile and a hug.

Monica ran to her mom. Anita said, "Monica, this is my friend Shannon. Shannon, this is my wonderful little daughter Monica."

Monica walked up to Shannon and shook her hand. "I am so happy to meet you," she said.

"Me too," Shannon said.

Grandma Salud brought everyone into the kitchen to have beans, rice and tortillas.

"You will sleep in my room tonight," Anita said.

"Thank you so much. This is so kind of you."

Everyone gathered in the living room to watch television.

"We can watch in English if you see something you like."

"No, I am learning Spanish. Let's watch Spanish." Shannon said.

Monica was in a chair drawing a picture. When it was finished she showed it to Shannon. "This is you, Mrs. Shannon," she said.

Shannon was astonished that such a young child could be such a talented artist.

Monica fell in love with Shannon and entertained her all evening. She shared her favorite stories and showed her favorite pictures. When Anita said, "Monica, it's bed time," Monica threw her arms around Shannon and said, "Please be here in the morning when I wake up. I want to make another picture."

The Santa Ana kept blowing and the fires in southern California kept threatening to burn more homes. Shannon spent four days with Anita's grandmother. When it was time to return home because the fire threat was gone, Shannon suggested that Anita bring Monica with them. Monica loved the idea.

Anita packed a suitcase and the three of them headed for Shannon's lovely home.

Shannon had always wanted a child. She was delighted to have a little girl living in her home.

They took Monica to Disneyland. She was so excited when all the Disney characters came to say hello to her. Disneyland had been Heavenly when she was there with Harold but it was even more spectacular seeing it through a child's eyes.

Another day they went to Sea World. Monica had never been there before and she was enchanted.

Shannon's refrigerator was covered with drawings by Monica.

Anita begged her not to buy too many toys for the little girl.

Unhappily Shannon obeyed her.

Shannon did a new will where she left the house to Anita .and Monica. Although she left most of her money to her father, Jeanette and Frank she left a nice sum to Anita and Monica.

Shannon was losing control of herself slowly but truly. She was afraid to go outside alone. Even in her own neighborhood she would get lost. At times she and Monica went walking and Monica could always find the house as long as they stayed in the neighborhood.

The day came when Shannon felt the way her mother had felt when she said she could not recognize her own hands or feet. She felt a stranger to her body.

One evening Shannon, Anita and Monica watched the story of a famous movie star who died with Alzheimer's. When the show ended there was a request for people to donate money to a Fund to Cure the disease. Shannon called the number and gave a large donation.

"It's good to know they are trying to cure this disease." She said. "I am in a place where I can touch earth, feel close to the sky, and see the sea."

"What did you say, Shannon?' Anita asked.

"Sometimes I don't know who I am but I always like me and I am glad you and Monica are here. God has blessed me with many beautiful people and places. My life is good even if it wanders from time to time. Even when I don't recognize my own hands I know that I am loved and love is all I've ever needed."

The End

Made in the USA